THE SWAY OF WINTER

Orla Murphy was born into a family of artists in County Cork. Her father was the sculptor Seamus Murphy, author of *Stone Mad*. After training as a conservator of books and manuscripts at Trinity College, Dublin, she worked freelance, chiefly for England's National Trust but also for Tinity College Library and various private collectors. She studied music at University College Cork with Seán Ó Riada and Aloys Fleischmann.

Her work has been short-listed for Hennessy Awards and for the Fish Short Story Competition, and has also been selected by David Marcus for *New Irish Writing* and *The Phoenix Short Stories Anthology* (1999), as well as being broadcast on BBC Radio 4 and on RTÉ Radio 1. Her poetry has appeared in *Cyphers* and other journals.

For my mother

The Sway of Winter

Orla Murphy

The Lilliput Press
Dublin

First published 2002 by
THE LILLIPUT PRESS LTD
62–63 Sitric Road, Arbour Hill,
Dublin 7, Ireland
www.lilliputpress.ie

A CIP record for this title is available from The British
Library.

1 3 5 7 9 10 8 6 4 2

ISBN 1 84351 002 2

ACKNOWLEDGMENTS
*Title from 'Winter Fields' by John Clare: 'O for a pleasant book
to cheat the sway of winter'. Lines on pages 35–6 from 'Clochard'
by Wislawa Szymborska.*

The Lilliput Press receives financial assistance from An
Chomhairle Ealaíon / The Arts Council of Ireland.

Set in 10 on 15 Hoefler Text
Printed in Ireland by Betaprint of Dublin

The Sway of Winter

I

So it is done. The last letter has been crumpled and twisted and tossed onto the flames. The square doorway of the little furnace holds the fire in a black frame. She throws in a handful of twigs and small branches that flare weakly. Lumps of driftwood tossed in next make a dull thump as the nest of kindling falls under their weight. A downdraught from the north wind sends smoke out into the room and she quickly closes the cast-iron door. The enamel surface is already warm and specks of soot and ash start to settle on the hotplate. She stands up and crosses to the sink to take the sponge from the basin and quickly wipes the stove's surface. More specks will settle, she knows, but she will wipe them off too. At last the letters and their weight will be lifted, light as air or ash and as easily moved. She opens the kitchen door and the room exhales smoke that is caught by the wind and swirled to the roof. She puts on her coat and goes out.

The house was on a finger of land on the north shore of the island with its back to the prevailing wind. At high tide it was surrounded by water, but the outlook from each window was bounded by land: the mainland, a low strip of pasture; other islands, some distant and high that disappeared in rain or fog, others close enough to reach by boat in minutes. The bulk of the island on which the house stood, Inis Breac, lay behind the western gable, overlooked by one small window.

Birgit felt the rocks through the heavy soles of her boots, finding ledges and natural steps with more ease each time she crossed them. Limpets and periwinkles crowded among the sea anemones whose red-wound mouths were shut tight until the next high tide. She reached the beach and walked its full curved length, seeing the tide deal out small waves that left fans of shells and pebbles after them. Beyond the low sandy shoulder was another beach and then a third from which the road, crisp and hard, rose and curved away from the sea through the meadows to the harbour. A pier with four iron rings was angled around a slip. Birgit walked along the narrow top of the pier wall, stepping over the empty rings, looking down on the few punts that sheltered on running moorings. She glanced over to the mainland where the pale landing-strip ran straight down the hill into the water. A further handful of boats was idling there, and in the fields above, a few cars were parked in the shelter of the hawthorn hedge. While she stood, a figure slammed a car door and moved down to the water to load several bags onto one of the boats. She saw the boat move before the sound of the engine reached across the strip of water, an almost calm path on a sea cross-hatched and shaken by the wind that filled out her coat like a sail and unwrapped her scarf into a rust-coloured pennant.

She walked the few yards between shoulder-high banks of grass and brambles uphill to the post office. An ice-cream sign and bottled gas drums flanked the door of the mobile home that was the island's source of food and fuel. As the only summer visitor who had stayed into autumn, she was conspicuous. One elderly man stood behind the counter, two more sat on barrels, their backs to the window where a sycamore tumbled light and shadow through the room like dice. Greetings were still progressing between the four of them when the postman entered. The canvas bags produced hardware, parcels, food and, tied with baler twine, a score of letters. Birgit held her breath as the postman sorted them. He came on a brown envelope for one of the old men. There were jokes about high living: an envelope with a window for your money to fly out. When the last envelope was face down on the others, Birgit breathed again. She bought a carton of milk and a handful of potatoes from the hundredweight in the sack that slumped like a torso against the counter.

As she left, the shopkeeper said, 'Wait, girl. He's stopped the letters and started on the gifts.' She took the package, pushed it in with the potatoes and walked back along the shore, face down. She didn't see the waders skip sideways from her, nor the other birds flung into the sky like handfuls of grain. Her feet thudded out of step with the waves. At the house she dropped the bag on the kitchen table and the parcel fell out. It was not Peter's handwriting. The name and address, in her grandmother's energetic loops and waves, covered most of the small rectangular surface of the package. With relief that rose in a warm pleasurable draught, she tore off the paper. Inside was a small black box. Its lid, three convex squares hinged, folded out to reveal a white interior and a second lid that unfolded opposite the first. She lifted them carefully, using her thumbs in the arced slots. Traces of mixed pigment still stained the insides of the lids, a flush of pink, specks of ultramarine, a rim of composite brown. The smell of the worn cubes of paint, twenty-seven of them, she had never been able to name. Medicinal? Astringent?

It reminded her of a time when she painted with that freedom that only small children know, when paint flowed easier than words. Eyes closed, she inhaled. Underneath the box was a fold of paper: 'I found this at the back of a cupboard. I am not sure

3

why I am sending it to you but you came into my thoughts as soon as I found it. Perhaps it is yours.' There was a smudge and the writing started again, using a different pen. 'Peter has just left. He was here for *so long*. I don't know how I could breathe for smoke from that deadly pipe. He sat in the corner, shaking his head. He sounded disappointed in you. How did you stand him for so long? He seems so old for a student. Graduate student. Mature student. Mature, like cheese. I asked him to come on to the balcony to see the trees in the park (they are all yellow now), but the idea of pleasure seemed to depress him and he went away taking his clouds of smoke with him, like a failed wizard.'

She held the paintbox, staring at the cubes of pigment, then went to the sink and poured a glass of water and drank. Cold struck her in the throat and forehead, low and painful. She tipped the remaining water into a saucer and put it on the table. She sat, rubbing her brow until the ache softened, then she dipped a finger in the water and moistened a square of green. Its dark socket yielded some colour and she stroked the letter with the tip of her forefinger. A plume like the wild spinach that she picked on the shore spread down the margin. She tried the black. At first it was palest grey, like a fin of the fish that she caught from the rocks, streaked onto the page. She dug into the black again and pressed the same ragged circle until the colour became that of periwinkles. She moved to the crimson, working the paint's crust until it yielded first pink and then the deep juice of ripe blackberries.

She went to the window and took a striped feather from a bowl of shells and stones. She put fresh water in the glass and scraped grains of ultramarine into it with the hard point of the feather. The grains released clouds, barely visible, that formed circles on the surface of the water. She stroked the water with the feather until it turned palest blue, then brushed the feather against the edge of the saucer, to drain it. On the flattened paper, she trailed the feather backwards and forwards until dark.

In the bright light of morning, the feather painting looked pallid and thin: a depthless sea. Only the page's edge gave it shape, a rectangular slice of pattern, empty of meaning or skill. Birgit opened the door and the warmth that bloomed inward drew her out. The day had declared a truce with autumn. The briny smell had softened and seaweeds on the tideline were already dry on top. She took off her shoes and socks. The water's cold raked at her feet. The tide was turning and, by afternoon, would have moved over hot sand. She sat on the low wall that circled the first beach and found among the rounded stones at her feet a flat one, speckled like a bird's egg, and a narrow red sliver that might once have been brick. With this she scratched curves and lines on the speckled stone, soon covering it. Then she took up another and tried to draw clouds. When she looked up again the clouds had moved and changed and her stone showed only ragged lines. She went back to the tideline to pick up a clump of seaweed. She shook it free then walked back to the cottage barefoot.

She searched in the table drawer among the knives and spoons and found a pencil. She took out her writing pad and started to draw. The pencil had a hard faint lead, gritty and ungiving. She tried to follow lines of the seaweed, noting the curves, the splayed ends of the fronds, the egg pouches, the minute limpets. She filled pages of the pad, but the seaweed, at first so easy in its shapelessness, had not yielded to her explorations. It lay on the table, containing its moistness, its density, like a secret. Every line she made seemed to move it farther away. She threw the pencil down and, tearing out the leaves, crumpled them. Going out to the sheltered end of the house she sat on the grass and, leaning against the gable, started to write.

Dear Oma,

Your paintbox arrived yesterday and I am trying to learn. My pencil is too hard and I have no brushes. I will go to town and find some. Here there is everything to paint or draw but I am impatient. I want to know the essence of each thing, instantly. Before, they were there, to admire or not, but now suddenly I want to understand them in all of their dimensions. It is like a hunger I did not know I had. It is how long since we used to paint together? Nine years? I remember sitting at your table with the light coming over my right shoulder, painting the things that were in my head. Now I am trying to see them as they are, without me. Almost, to listen to them. But the harder I try, the more they retreat into their own mystery. I wish you were well enough to write to me, then you could scold me for complaining. You give me a gift and I find it unlocks my lack of skill. I did better drawing as a child but I will learn, I will, somehow.

I can see you sitting on the balcony (I hope it is still warm enough for you) with the tops of the trees waving like a signal between you and Mum and you sometimes glancing across to her apartment to see if she is on her balcony. I hope you can still manage to stay in your own place. I will say this to her myself but I know Papa will take your side if she starts to worry out loud.

Everyone is gone from here. The island (which is very quiet when there are people around) has become loud again with its own voice. The waves sound as though they are coming to the door. The

6

swallows fly in the front and out the back, from light to light. The wind moves the reeds in the marsh where sometime the sea will make another island. I can hear it hiss. I would miss the sounds of children playing on the shore and the movement of the boats but for the endless music of different birds and insects and, of course, the sea.

But I am contradicted as I write. There is a boat. I can just hear the engine. The regular ferry comes later. The fishermen are too far away. Who can this be?

Please tell Mum she was right about Peter. I have asked him to stop writing. He says all he wants is an explanation for my leaving. There is no kind way to tell him that if I had stayed another day, I would have suffocated. I used to find his solemnity charming, as though he were playing at being a lawyer, with his waistcoat and watch-chain and habit of pausing before answering. On the day he told me (he almost whispered) that he intended to become a Judge, I reacted as to a calamity: he had the certainty of one who could not imagine anything else. I do not have to tell you how much room for doubt there is in my life, you know already. I tried to tell him something of that but he did not understand. I should be a Defendant all my life. So I hope I have had the last of his letters.

It grows too warm to write. I shall go for a swim. And when I have progressed I will send you a painting of my house with its peeling walls and lichened slate.

Love, Birgit.

2

I had become the kind of person I used to avoid on the street: roaring, crying, suddenly catching the eye of a stranger and trying to tell him something, hair tangled and staring, pockets ripped, tie (when I still wore one) a cliché of askewness, snot-smeared cuffs, half-eaten, half-spewed meals become one soup on shirt, jacket, trousers. But that was nothing compared to the face. Oh Christ, the face. I learned how to avoid my eye long before others did. Their turned-away faces reminded me of what I could not bear to see.

There are dozens of words for drink in *Roget's Thesaurus*. The euphemisms are innumerable. This I learned when I finally sobered up. That hardly describes it: going from one depth of ugliness and pain to another. The first is public, the second private and lonely. Before, the emptiness was peopled with enemies and friends, an endless cast to call up or banish, willing co-conspirators in my whims. After, there was no one but me to realize that I had killed the whole cast of ghosts, their mortal selves long gone, enemies first and then, slowly, friends. Self-pity, the only survivor, was banished too. I had to carry my own dead weight.

The face that now met me in the mirror (I had progressed that far) was a battered version of my own. The skin permanently chalky, the flesh above my eyes sagged into twin loops, like curtains sheltering eyes that have become, yes, another cliché, pickled onions. Glasses helped a little. The hair has treated the whole twenty years as an embarrassing episode: wavy, thick, golden, a burnished lid, ludicrously out of keeping with the ruins on which it sat, like a gleaming helmet on a battlefield the morning after a rout. This is the face my son sees.

He lit the first cigarette of the day. He had turned the sign on the door of the shop to 'Open' and raised the blind in the window. Pale sun fell at an angle on the covers of the books and Dundee, the cat, was settled on a centrefold portrait of Mata Hari, her sultry pose obliterated by this orange fur comma.

He went back through the narrow room lined with books to a small kitchen where the kettle was boiling. As he returned to the counter in the shop and set down a mug of coffee, he saw a station-wagon blur to a stop on the double yellow lines. The back was a thicket of gilded legs, polished handles and striped upholstery. More furniture was crammed into the trailer, lashed down under a tarpaulin. Before he had a chance to pick up the newspaper, the door opened and a tall woman with white curly hair stepped out. He opened the paper with a sharp crack and read. He turned the pages without lowering it. By the time his cigarette was burned to the tip and he had to lay down the paper, she and the furniture were gone into the house next door, where a sign-painter had spent two days lettering 'Bective Antiques' in gold upon the plate-glass window.

He lit another cigarette and waited until its feathery comfort soothed his lungs before he got up and scanned the shelves. Gaps were beginning to appear. The cloth-bound copy of White's *Natural History of Selborne* went yesterday. The buyer, a woman with mismatched eyes, didn't want it wrapped, and as it disappeared into her bag he saw it in Pollock's hand forty-one years earlier and heard the silence in the school hall, before the leafy crackle of applause. The buyer (her eyes were not different in colour, one was fractionally higher than the other) did not read the gothic-lettered 'for excellence in nature studies'. She tilted her head (to even up her vision? Give the lower eye a better chance?) and snapped the bag shut.

The gap where it stood was bisected diagonally by the next book. He tried to straighten it but it fell, first one way, then the other. He took it down and opened it. 'To Sadie from Geoff, Christmas 1970, with thanks.' Even as children, she'd always wanted to play hospital, always been the nurse, with him, her younger brother, as patient. It seemed to him that a smell of hospital, antiseptic with an implication of decay, rose from its pages. She would have added it to the library that was trundled around the wards on trolleys. As Matron what use could she have had for mere books? Distractions. Paltry tokens of thanks for her care of his son who sat, wordless, watching him with large anxious eyes, the packet of sweets clutched unopened in one hand, the other gripping her arm until she released him gently saying, 'I need my reading glasses, Simon, would you fetch them?' When the child had hurried from the room, grateful for his escape, Sadie would turn to Geoff. While his hands shook and his eyes went into brief, uncertain focus, she could not say, 'Your son needs you ... he should see more of you.' Only once, provoked to thoughtlessness by a very long absence, she had said, 'It won't do any good, you drowning your sorrows.' And then she had bitten her lip while he closed his eyes and saw yet again the sunlight glitter on the water that streamed down off the car: a weed-strewn metal shell with Clare and Rosie inside, still and white as pearls.

Sadie had taken care of Simon until he was grown up and

then, in her last illness, Simon took care of her. She died in his house one afternoon in May while Geoff lay on a table-tomb in St Mary de la Poer churchyard, nursing a bottle.

The bulk of the small estate had gone to Simon and Becky, but Sadie had given him one last chance. It was the absence of conditions on the annuity that had shocked him into sobriety. The books, hers and his, unused but not uncared-for, had followed on, a prompt, a clue to her thoughts. Had she guessed that he had once wanted to have a bookshop? A sister can know you better than you know yourself. Dundee had been thrown in for good measure: a scrap of life, a discreet presence. He gently closed the book and put it back on the shelf, moving its companion to support it. On the shelf above there were three or four gaps, more on the shelf below. He scanned the two longer walls. The gaps drew the eye more than the books, the deal shelves still resinous and white, and already he had to think about stock. Bits of his past turned over and wanted by strangers. He thought of the woman. She didn't want his past, just the book itself, its felty usedness: it had looked at home in her hands.

He picked up the newspaper again. The local events had a soothing irrelevance: squash championships, cross-country running, pub quizzes. He turned to the ads. Something caught his eye amid the scores of bungalows. 'Country House Auction. All Contents. The last of the Delamere family whose great-grandfather is pictured left' – a jowly fox-hunting face – 'after two hundred years continual ... Sat. next, 2 pm.' He cut out the ad.

The auction was held in a shed behind the square stucco house that had once been a rectory. Geoff walked from the town along the narrow straight street of former shops where curtains were a backdrop to display windows of bare shelves and once or twice a plant or vase of plastic flowers. Traffic speeded up where the street ended and the broad road from town widened. It passed houses standing in large neat gardens, then fields. He met no one, walking on the soft margin. Under a bent concrete paling he saw a wet tangle of flowers, cellophane and purple synthetic ribbon looped into a rosette. The card read, 'Martin, 19. Always, Mam and Dad.'

A hand-scrawled sign pointed to the rectory. People drifted through the shed poking at rolls of carpet, furniture, boxes of incomplete sets of china, glasses, decanters without stoppers. The paintings stacked against the walls had recently had a smear of varnish or gold paint on the frames. There was a smell of dust, · mould and sour earth. At three o'clock the auctioneer (Geoff recognized his landlord), conspicuous in suit and striped shirt, began a hearty welcome. The shed filled up with standing figures, grey in the gloom, faces pale in the light that edged through grimy skylights. Interest was shown in the dining-table, a battered mahogany oval. Iron-spotted linen lay in crooked piles. Several women tussled quietly over sets of fish knives. Tobacco-coloured paintings, scored and peeling, went for £5. Behind Geoff there was a snuffling. A large man sagged on the lower steps of a ladder. The jowls of the fox-hunting face shook as he grunted 'bloody waste of time' and lumbered from the shed.

The auction ended. The auctioneer gathered his papers and winked at Geoff. 'And we all know why you're here. The Library, so-called, is behind you, 'twasn't worth listing.' A few cardboard boxes were heaped under the ladder. 'If you can get anything out of that lot you're a better man than me.' He lowered his voice. 'Anything of value in this dump went on the drink or the geegees years ago. Take 'em away with you.' He considered Geoff. 'You'll have no car.' His earlobes bulged upwards and shone pink. 'But your new neighbour will see you right.' Waving his catalogue, he set off across the room and returned with a tall woman, nudging her through the Delamere remnants with one hand on her elbow. Geoff and the woman looked at one another. 'Now don't tell me you haven't met Mrs Thompson. She's got the shop next to you. Antiques.' She had pale grey eyes and brown lined skin. She looked at him. 'I'm sorry?' Her tone was not warm. 'Sure she won't mind at all.' The auctioneer hoisted a box under each arm. 'Mrs T.'ll have plenty of space.' Geoff watched as his sturdy rump vanished out of the shed, then turned to the tall woman. 'Of course you must let me help,' she said. 'That's very kind,' he began, but she was already rooting out a box and carrying it to the door. Geoff followed them, the damp carton a dead weight on his chest. Mrs Thompson was sitting in the driving-seat with the engine running. Geoff leaned down to look in the open passenger door.

'This is an imposition.'

'No it's not.' She was looking into the rear-view mirror. He put the box into the boot then shut it and sat in to the car. 'It's that frightful man.' She turned the car. Geoff could see the auctioneer in the wing mirror, grinning, his striped paunch ballooned in the curved surface.

She drove fast out of the gate and down the narrow road to the junction. Geoff groped in his pocket then saw the red circle and cancelled cigarette stuck to the dashboard. He sat back and looked at her profile and then at her strong hands on the wheel. 'I'm afraid you've had a wasted journey,' he tried. They turned on to the main road. 'Chancer. Dragging me out here for that pile of rubbish.' Geoff glanced back at the boxes. She made a face at him. 'Not your stuff. No, I'm glad you found something. Books?'

'I hope so.'

She gave a shout of laughter. 'Maybe I should have talked to you before I bothered going out today. You get all your stock from auctions?'

'I brought it with me.'

'From England?'

'Suffolk. But I'm having to look around for more.'

The traffic grew more dense as they came to the roundabout. All roads were directed through the town. They passed the church, the library and arts centre. He longed for a cigarette. For diversion he said, 'And you?', hoping he sounded interested.

'Oh I'm trying a change from the city. It doesn't suit my sister. Her health. The country would be best but I've got to earn a living. We both liked the way the houses backed on to the river. And it's handy for the country. She likes to walk, on good days. Now –'

They were at his door. His offer of tea was declined. 'Olivia doesn't know her way round yet. I can't leave her for too long. Come and have a cup with us any time. Tomorrow.' She had carried in some of the boxes and stood in the doorway. She interrupted his thanks. 'Only positive part of the day,' she said and the lines of her face fused into a smile. He watched as she drove off and parked on the other side of the street, against the flow of traffic. He found his cigarettes and lit up. Then he opened the nearest box. Schoolbooks. Pages pulp-soft. Hall and Knight's *Geometry* lying at the bottom, angles warped. He put the box out in the shed that leaned against the kitchen and opened the next one. Maps. The calico showed on the folds but the detailed vastness of the countries was still clear. He slotted them into the Travel shelf, putting the ones that would not fit on top.

He was unpacking the third box when he noticed the red blink of the answering machine. There was a message from Simon. His voice was stilted, as always on the phone, the aural equivalent of avoiding someone's eye. He had the politeness of a stranger or a distant relation. Geoff wondered if he would ever manage the word 'Dad'. To avoid the direction his thoughts were taking, he returned the call and was relieved to hear Becky's recorded voice, cheerful and soft.

He cleared his throat. 'It's me,' he said. 'Thanks. Lunch'd be great. See you tomorrow.'

He emptied another box. Manuals. Horse-riding, polo, equine maladies, cars, aeroplanes, speedboats. Wedged inside one was a small wartime book on toy-making. He put it aside and shelved the others, then looked at it again. Line-drawings of a rocking horse, an ark and a slide gave no clue to its presence. It was clean, without inscription, never opened, perhaps never used. He tried to imagine Delamere as a child finding this book, perhaps trying to persuade an adult to make one of the toys. The image eluded him.

The last box contained a miscellany. He put the mildewed ones in the bin, turned over the rest and found one with light boards covered in pale blue paper. Very gently he opened it. *Ireland, Its Scenery and Character etc.* by Mr and Mrs S.C. Hall. The paper was heavy and white, the print generous. An original? First edition? He checked in an antiquarian catalogue then wrapped the book in clean brown paper and set it aside to read before placing it on the 'Rare' shelf where its unlettered spine would be a magnet to collectors. The rest he distributed on the bargain table, then he picked up a history of clocks and put it in an envelope, addressing it to Mrs Thompson, with thanks. Leaving the Open sign on the door (he would be only a few seconds), he went out.

The pristine glass of 'Bective Antiques' reflected 'Moore's Meats' from the other side of the street, obscuring the dark gleam of polished wood and damask. He opened the door, ready to place the envelope on the nearest surface, but the clang of a bell stopped him. He hesitated, then a woman appeared slowly from behind a curtain. He stared: the same curly hair but silver

15

and fine. The same face but thin, with translucent skin.

She smiled. 'You're looking for Jenny. I'm her sister.' She held out her hand and he took it. Her touch was light as a child's. 'Is that –?' She looked at the envelope.

'Oh, oh yes.' He let go of her hand then thrust the envelope into it, reddening as he did so. 'She might. You might. It's about clocks,' he said, and glanced around as if in proof. Her smile broadened. 'Jenny will be delighted.' He backed to the door. 'It's just a thank-you for the lift.' The bell drowned his words as he opened the door and turned into the street.

He reached his kitchen and lit a cigarette. He must have appeared demented: stammering, blushing. He needed a glass in his hand, just to hold. He poured water into a tumbler and sat at a table. Drawing heavily on the cigarette, he calmed. It could have been worse. They could have appeared together and he might have panicked completely, thinking that the illusion was his own creation. But they would have been wearing different clothes. Fool. How could he prepare himself against the endless punishments of sobriety? He took a sip of water. Its dullness chastened him. Poor woman. He had probably frightened her, taking her hand instead of the book. He rose slowly and poured the water down the sink. A fly walked up the windowpane and he brushed at it. It rose briefly then settled in the same place. He thought of her amused face, her quiet self-possession. No, he had not frightened her.

He opened the back door and walked down the short slope to the river. High grass and some overgrown shrubs led to the unfenced brink. On the other side, broad flat fields were grazed by cattle. The rear of the main street bordered the left side and hills rose beyond the pasture, curving around to the right. It had the still, contained peace of a forgotten space. He turned and went back to his door and heard music, faint, orchestral, coming from the Thompsons'. He listened, eyes shut, for a moment, then went in.

Sunday morning. The streets had a sibilance: the sound of footsteps. Traffic noises from the area of the church were distant as Geoff walked to the supermarket and chose apples, a melon and a box of dates, still sticky on their branch. The air was so warm that the door had been left ajar. The green and white awning kept the window, brilliant as some surreal jewellers, in shadow. The buckets and spades that hung by the door of the newsagents had been replaced with net bags of footballs. He collected his paper and bought a bag of sweets. He hesitated for a long time in the off-licence while the man at the counter gazed dreamily into the street, his fingers tapping the rhythm of a song he heard in his head. Merlot, Sauvignon, Pinot Noir. Any bottle was the same as any other. Geoff went back to the first one on the row.

He had hardly reached the outskirts of the town when he was hailed by Becky. She had driven in to collect him. 'It's much too hot to walk. And besides, you're laden.'

'Only a couple of miles,' he said, gratefully sitting in to the car. The air from the open window brought a warm perfume from the fields. Her arms, resting on the wheel, were brown where she had turned up the sleeves of her shirt. The car was full of toys and gardening tools. There was a smell of dog.

'Tom and Stevie are so excited. We're going to Inis Breac for a picnic. You don't mind? It's a pet day. We mayn't get another.'

In front of the house was a vegetable garden running up to a low wall. Inside the wall, on a patch of grass, lay a boy, his head resting on one arm, as he drew huge, uneven circles on the back of a strip of wallpaper, held down with four stones. He looked up and grinned.

'Say hello, Stevie,' said Becky. 'Simon's in his workshop trying to finish a set of chairs for some posh hotel and Tom, where's Tom?' Stevie waved towards the bottom of the garden and continued drawing.

Inside the house was dim. Thick walls and small windows made pastel colours of the patchwork on the settle and the flowers in a pint glass on the table. Becky went into the back kitchen and Geoff sat on the edge of the settle.

A smell of baking came through the open doorway as she gathered food and talked. Geoff took the book on toy-making out of his pocket, leaned over and put it on the corner of the table. Becky came in and reached up for a basket hanging from one of the rafters and started to fill it with food. 'Stevie's just started school,' she said, looking into the dresser for glasses. 'Of course it's new for Tom too and he still misses his friends. I suppose seven's not the best age for big changes, like moving house and country, but what is?' Geoff could not think of an answer.

'But they are happy enough,' she said, slotting the tumblers into a tower which she started to wrap when Simon came through the open front door.

'Your dad brought some wine and fruit. Wasn't that nice?' she said, in a louder voice. Simon glanced at the bags.

'Mm? Oh, right,' he said, 'and this?' He picked up the book.

With his back to the light and the beams almost touching his head, Simon seemed to eclipse the day, even to have appropriated all the air in the room. Becky was still, watching him. The book looked shabby in his hand.

'Just something I found.' Geoff tried not to sound apologetic. Simon flicked through it and stopped at an illustration.

'I had a wooden train once,' he said quietly.

'Oh?'

'Bit bigger than this. Four carriages. Green and a bell.'

Becky looked at his face carefully then said, 'Did Geoff make it?'

'I reckon.'

'And what became of it?'

'Dunno.' He closed the book and put it down. He headed for the door. 'I'll round up the boys.'

Becky's face was pink. 'He's all right really,' she said. 'It'll take time.' She looked at Geoff, shrunk back into a corner of the settle. 'He doesn't know what to say.'

'Neither do I,' said Geoff.

'You were embarrassed. I shouldn't have spoken.'

'Not embarrassed. Afraid. I can't remember making anything for him.'

The colour died away slowly from her face. 'It'll take time,' she said again, too emphatically.

Tom and a red setter came hurtling into the room and dashed towards the stairs. Becky called them back and, while the dog ran around the table, tail flailing, Tom looked up at Geoff and said, 'Hello, Granddad.' It had an experimental sound. Geoff smiled at the clear alert face. 'You going swimming then?' he said. Tom looked at his mother. 'Can I?' 'Better find your trunks.' He raced up the stairs. 'I can do two lengths,' he shouted through the banisters.

Geoff sat in the back of the car with Tom holding a butterfly net out of the window. Stevie was upright between them, not touching either. The setter breathed down their necks. Simon drove in silence.

When the car stopped at the ferry field, Tom shouted that he had caught a butterfly, climbing up through the window to look at it. Becky and Simon smiled at one another.

Geoff was last down to the water's edge. Simon held the boat steady and Geoff put out a hand to help the boys aboard but they threw themselves into it without heeding the narrow gap that quaked immeasurably between it and the pier. Becky stepped in next with the basket held up in both hands, but when Geoff started to follow her, Simon moved aboard ahead of him. Geoff hesitated until the ferryman reached out and tugged at his arm, then he scrambled in, trying not to look down, focusing on the paintwork, the oarlocks, the robust motor, and sat gritting his teeth against the boat's sly motion. He sighed, started to relax and fixed his gaze on the island, but saw peripherally every move that the children made and gripped the seat to prevent his hands from reaching out involuntarily in unwanted impulses of rescue.

The ferryman pointed the punt upstream into the current that then bore them comfortably down to Inis Breac pier. Tom explained this to Stevie who was gazing into the sky. Rex sat, a copper figurehead, in the prow, waiting to be first to set foot on shore, and as soon as they landed he arrowed up the hill with Tom running after him, clutching his swimsuit and towel roll and a football. Geoff and Becky followed with rugs and towels and Simon carried Stevie on his shoulders and the basket in one hand. Stevie held the net above his head until his arms tired.

The island gave them a new, freer air, and they stepped briskly up the road that led past the post office and swung around and down to the largest beach. Simon, burdened, strode past Becky and Geoff who strolled, collecting a hatful of blackberries from the brambles that looped along the stone walls, and when they rounded the last bend and looked down, they could see him and the boys at the water's edge, with Rex herding the waves.

Geoff lay back on the gentle slope of the beach and watched the four figures move in the water. The football bounced hard on the surface and the dog plied earnestly, changing direction with endless patience as arms, voices and spray flashed about his head. Geoff lay motionless, watching, hearing a word, a name, hoping to catch something from the unspecific memory that weighed on him. But what he saw immediately before him was like a news-reel: something vaguely familiar that gave moments of recognition too brief to be certain about, too universal to be claimed as his own. Was that what unused memory did, moved randomly, focusing on things without will, gleaning fragments from lives unchosen, while the real energy was spent on avoidance? *A void dance.*

'Sorry?' Becky, leaning on her elbows, gazing down to sea, turned her head to look at him. 'You said something?'

Geoff shook his head. 'Never mind my ramblings.'

She raised her eyebrows.

'It's just being on my own. I don't hear myself. Probably talk all the time.' He tried to laugh.

'We are a bit of a crowd,' she said. The boys were running up from the water. 'And noisy.'

She wrapped towels around them as they shuddered and leaned against her.

Geoff wanted to say something, make some grateful denial, something, anything that would express his wish to move towards her kindness. She glanced at him. 'You could put the food out,' she said suddenly, casually. 'We have hungry tigers here.'

Geoff lifted the basket to the edge of the rug and unwrapped the mugs and plates. He set out cheese on waxed paper and chicken with lettuce on a board. He poured fruit juice into glasses for the boys and himself and wine for Simon and Becky. He found the tomatoes and the salt and the foil parcel of smoked mackerel. As he smelled the food and touched the wrappings, he heard the voices of the children wondering if a horseshoe beach was longer than a swimming-pool oblong. He drew a deep breath and started to cut the bread. Each stroke of the blade sliced through his pent-up fog of deadened memory. Kneeling on a fringed rug, towelling a child's hair, her own hair hanging loose, wearing a white dress with cornflowers at the hem, had been Clare. Clare and Rosie. The close texture of the bread almost silenced the knife.

Tom peered out of his towel. 'Here comes Dad,' he said. Geoff looked up at his son. 'Feed the hungry,' said Simon, salt water making rivulets through the hair on his legs. Becky put food on plates for the boys. Simon sat on a towel and looked towards Geoff, still holding the bread. 'What's the matter? No appetite? You should swim. Clear away all those cobwebs.' Hearty as a stranger, he bit into a tomato. Geoff offered bread then put chicken and salad on a plate.

When they had finished, Simon collected mugs and plates and washed them in the sea. Tom and Stevie carried them back and wiped them dry and Becky packed them in the basket. Simon stretched out and fell asleep. The boys wandered off, talking and investigating. On the low wall that bordered the beach they found speckled stones with orange-red lines and marks drawn on them. They invented a plot, scratching lines on other stones and leaving them at carefully paced distances. Geoff could see them, measuring out the pattern in their bare feet, stooping down and arranging the stones. When they came back, he was almost asleep. Becky was lying on her back with her straw hat on her face. They stood at his feet.

'We want to explore.'

Geoff looked at Becky and Simon.

'Would they let you?'

Tom was silent.

'There might be a monster,' said Stevie. 'We found secret signs.'

'Never,' said Geoff, getting to his feet.

'I told him,' said Tom, 'but he wouldn't believe me.'

They ran ahead of him, wings of sand at their bony heels. He inspected the stones they had found, seeing cloud shapes and waves, then walked after them, stopping to examine their own patterns and runes.

'Will it work? Our magic?' asked Tom.

Geoff thought. He turned to the sea. He shaded his eyes and turned around towards the west where the sun was declining. Then he turned back and pointed east. 'Came from there. Not a monster, just a messenger.' He stared at the chalky red lines. 'Can't make out what it says. Best be on the safe side.' He picked up the stones and set off for the sea. They followed. He handed them the stones. 'Now. Set them there.' He pointed to the water's edge, where the tide was almost at its height. They put the stones down and backed away, staring, as the water crept towards them. Geoff set off briskly. 'We'll check on our way back.' The boys followed him, looking over their shoulders to where the stones lay surrounded by sand, visible markers, not yet touched by the water. Tom went back for the butterfly net. They scrambled over walls, through bracken, losing their footing, stumbling upwards, with butterflies and cinnabar moths rushing ahead. Tom stalked them, flailing the huge net, while Stevie turned over leaves, looking for caterpillars. They reached the top of the hill and Geoff sat on the rough ground and lit a cigarette. He could see the boys and the setter moving down the short slope to the next beach. Tom shouted up to him, 'Here's another ocean.' Geoff climbed down and lay on the warm sand while the boys searched the water's edge. He looked past them to where the water became deep green and then grey. He saw a shape, a dark gleam, quite still in the water, a seal's head? Then it moved and he could see arms and the ripple of feet. He watched as the swimmer rounded the headland and disappeared. Finding no secret messages, the boys moved on. Geoff buried his cigarette and followed.

The next beach was small, hardly more than a couple of hundred yards in length. Geoff walked its curved edge until he came to smooth rocks where he leant against the warm stone, still bright in the western light. Stevie brought him shells which he put in his pocket. Tom was building a castle with a moat using the butterfly-net pole and then his hands. As they worked, Geoff dozed, accommodating his back to the shape of the rock. The sea sucked pebbles from between the rocks. A movement, a clink, just louder than the rest alerted him and he craned his head to see the cause. A woman stepped out of the sea. Her hair was as close as skin about her head and water drained down between her breasts. She did not see Geoff, too startled to move, as she wiped her face with one hand and stood for a moment with the sea reaching just above her ankles. Then she turned around to look out at the horizon, and the sun, reflecting up from the water, made diamonds of the drops that hung all over her body and threw a halo of yellow light about her legs, between them and around her arms and shoulders. Tom shouted something and Geoff turned. The boys were walking towards him. When he glanced back again the woman had moved away and was walking the narrow causeway that led to a small house.

The water had spilled into the moat and vanished. A wave reached towards the castle and fell short. The next fell further below and the next. Just as Geoff was about to say 'Tide's going out', two waves converged and rushed over the castle. They watched. It did not happen again. 'Time to go and see your stones,' Geoff said.

Tom trailed the butterfly net in the water, catching ribbons of bright green weed. Stevie plodded on. At the hill, he sat down. Geoff hoisted him up on his shoulders and struggled up the slope. When Tom shouted that he could see the stones, Stevie slipped down and ran. They bent over and Geoff stopped, watching the two brown heads together. 'The sea has taken back the message,' shouted Tom.

'We're all right then, are we?' enquired Stevie. They both turned, still crouched together, and looked up at Geoff. 'Reckon so,' he said.

They rose and raced towards their parents. Simon was standing, looking out to sea. Becky sat with her hands behind her head.

'It's time we went. Ferry'll be going soon.' Simon was gathering up the towels from the wall, shaking out sand and picking off bits of seaweed.

The procession set off again with Stevie on Simon's shoulders and Tom bouncing the ball. Geoff carried the basket and towels. Becky brought the rugs and the net and Rex padded after them, head down. The car, despite being in the shade of the hawthorn, released a wall of heat. Stevie fell asleep and began to slip sideways against Geoff. With great care, Geoff eased the child around until his head rested comfortably. Then he took Stevie's hand in his and lay back, seeing the smoky dusk gather above the hedgerows. From time to time he looked down at the sleeping face and once touched the child's hair, feeling the warmth of the scalp and the smallness of the head and his heart contracted with longing.

After supper Simon put the boys to bed. The sound of his voice, reading to them, came as a murmur through the ceiling, while Geoff helped Becky with the washing-up.

Then he went down to the end of the garden to smoke a cigarette. It was almost dark. The red of the cigarette and an occasional reflection from the narrow stream in the field were the only light near him. The windows of the house were yellow, glowing with the light of lives savoured and cherished.

A window in the kitchen opened as Becky put out a moth and

he heard their voices in conversation, easy now that they were alone. If he should enter the kitchen their talk would stop for a fraction of a second and then resume on a different note. Becky would turn to look at him and Simon would continue putting away the plates but with more energy. No Sadie to send him on an invented errand.

Geoff drew hard on his cigarette and found that the tip had snapped. He dropped it and pressed it out on the soft grass. The door opened and Simon crossed the garden to his workshop. Geoff waited a few minutes and then went towards the house slowly.

In the kitchen, Becky was sitting at the table.

'I'll be off then.' His voice, coming suddenly, sounded harsh. She insisted on driving him and, dragging on her cardigan, picked up her keys from the dresser. 'I'd like to.' She stopped and looked at him. 'Do let me.'

They were on the main road when she spoke.

'Things going well in the shop?'

'Mm. Yes. Had a find at a sale. Lovely little book, first edition, publisher's binding and all.'

'That's good, is it?'

'Well, y'know, collectable.' Becky's interest in books stopped at gardening. He could not imagine how to describe the feeling that the modest volume had given him.

'What was it about?'

'Travel.'

She laughed. 'We'll not be doing much of that for a while. Too busy settling in.'

'Of course. But you're happy here?'

'It's coming right. The boys are getting on fine in school and I'm happy wherever Simon is but I think he ... I'm not sure yet.'

'Business worries?'

26

'No, that's going well. He's just a worrier, I suppose. Always anxious.'

Pointless to say, 'And I'm part of those worries.' Pointless and selfish. He watched the relentless slip of the broken white line. He should not have followed them and settled like a cloud on their lives. The needle of self-pity pricked him and to quell it he spoke suddenly.

'Anything I can do? To help, I mean?'

'No, of course not. But thanks.'

Her reply, as abrupt as his question, gave them a moment's complicity and they glanced at one another and smiled, embarrassed.

They had reached the town. She pulled the car into the kerb noiselessly.

He opened the door. 'Thank you for everything.'

'You'll come next Sunday?'

'Maybe not next Sunday. I'll phone. It was a wonderful day.' He got out of the car.

'Don't forget your blackberries.' She handed him a glass bowl from the back seat. 'The last of the year.'

3

At the back of the newsagents, the stationery section and art materials had a low-ceilinged room to themselves. Birgit chose pencils, brushes, a large pad of heavy paper and a putty rubber. A box of charcoal sticks felt too light to have anything in it, but when she pushed open the flap it was filled with black twigs that creaked when she touched them.

In the street, the wind that had blown the ferry off course was channelled between tall rows of houses, cutting horizontally and pressing her waterproofs stiffly against her. She stepped off the footpath over the water that filled the gutters and crossed to look into the window of the antique shop. Above a sideboard hung a painting. She made a hood of her hands and peered at it. It was a landscape showing a valley between two mountains, the sky descending into a V. Straining her eyes, she thought she could see a river uncoiling through the shadowy floor of the valley. She caught sight of a man perched on the edge of a desk. He was brushing a picture frame, then holding it up and blowing the dust from the crevices. He held it up, saw her looking at him and smiled at her. She stepped back, bumping into a woman with a push-chair and a child, transfixed beneath a clear plastic dome. The man watched, eyebrows raised in mock sorrow as she walked away.

Rain flooded down the window of the bookshop. She could make out the shape of an orange cat alseep on the cover of a book. She opened the door and hesitated on the step as water dripped from the hem of her coat. A smell of coffee and cigarettes reached her as the man behind the counter said, 'Never mind the floor. Come in.' He was sitting behind a pile of books, reading a newspaper with a cigarette in an ashtray beside him. 'Kettle's just boiled. Like a mug?'

'Thank you.'

He pointed towards a row of hooks behind the door. 'You can leave your things there.'

She took off her sou'wester and turned towards the door, then looked back as he gave a muffled yelp. He was rubbing his hand.

'Just spilled my coffee.' He rose and went through a door at the back of the shop. 'Won't be a tick.'

She unfastened her raincoat and hung it on a hook, then wandered along the shelves, inhaling the fustiness of the books cut through by the sharpness of the pine shelving.

She stopped at the photography shelf, took down a book called *Women and Land* and leafed slowly through it. 'Working in a tin mine, Bolivia', was the caption on a picture of a woman dwarfed by rocks and boulders, scooping something from a crude tray above a round improvised bath of muddy water. She turned to another page: 'Harvesting sugar cane, West Bengal'. The image was a tangle of lines, blades of sugar cane that rose above the woman whose fierce labour, hacking at the stalks with a sickle or a machete, was etched in every line. Birgit turned the page again. The foreground of the next photograph ('Loading Rice, Ghana') showed three huge bags packed and tied at the neck, and behind them a woman hoisting a fourth onto her head. She was very slender and had a cloth wrapped around her body, weighted down at the back by a sleeping child.

Disturbed by the pictures, their beauty so much at odds with the struggle shown in each, she didn't hear anything until the mug of coffee was set down on the table beside her. When she turned, the bookseller had already retreated behind the counter.

'Carry on,' he said, 'don't mind me,' and he picked up the newspaper. He was thin. His white hands held the paper like a shield before his face. His hair was that of a man in his thirties but she guessed him to be nearer to sixty. He lowered the paper and gave a smile that looked unpractised, tentative.

'Weather for ducks.'

'Yes. I like to swim too but not in this.' The rain had made the street so dark that cars had turned on their lights.

'Yes,' he said, dropping his glance.

'But I stay on Inis Breac, I am used to water,' she tried.

He nodded, looking tense, even, she thought, embarrassed.

'I'll take this.' She put the book on the counter and went to lift the waterproofs from the hook under which a pool had spread. By the time she found her money and worked her way into her coat, the book had been wrapped and placed inside two plastic bags. She went out into the street where the yellow of her coat shone briefly before being eclipsed by clouds of rain.

The sea was calming by the time she caught the ferry and the wind had died. The ferryman helped her on board and passed her in her bags. Then, from its clips under the centre thwart, he took a golf umbrella and erected it gravely over her head. Facing forward, her back to him, she held her breath until the engine started and then she laughed, swaying with the boat, tactful under the umbrella, all the way to the island.

The high tide had almost covered the rocky causeway that led to her house and water splashed into her boots. She had to light the stove, dry her waterproof with an old towel and stuff her boots with newspaper before she could unpack her bags.

30

She opened the drawing pad and took up one of the new pencils. With the pad propped on her knee and resting on the edge of the table, she started to make an outline of the enamel kettle. The handle was lopsided, the spout wrong: too thin. She rubbed out and tried again. If she made the lines parallel, the spout should be right. It wasn't. She rubbed out again and again. Eventually she made a spout that looked better but still did not look like the one on the kettle. The paper was grey with smudged erasures and ghost lines. She put down her pencil and got up and walked around the table to see from every angle, but the kettle had no angles. Its lines curved out of sight. The shine of reflected light moved with her and disappeared when she came between it and the window.

She sharpened her pencil and made a fine point, rolling the lead on sandpaper. She drew several handles. They looked not bad. She tried a spout and another and another. They were irregular but not with the irregularity of the kettle's spout. She drew the lid, then she drew the whole kettle again. The lid, the handle, the spout did not fit well together. Her first attempt looked better than her last. She put her head down on the page and closed her eyes. When she opened them, the kettle loomed dark and shiny, an alien shape. She stood up, stretched, saw and heard the rain and spray flung at the windows. She put a lump of wood into the stove, filled the kettle with water and set it on the hotplate.

She lifted down a string of onions, the last of her harvest, from a nail above the window. The skins rustled as she laid the plait on the table and chose a pencil. She drew fast. The roundness of the onions, their withered necks and desiccated roots, yielded to her concentrated stare. She tried the charcoal. It broke under the pressure of her hand. Using the short piece, she snagged and pushed it on the paper. She held it flat on the page and made broad patches. She forgot the onions in her curiosity to see what the charcoal could do. Her hands became black and she rubbed that onto the page too. Every inch of the page was covered with demonic swirls and blurs. She laid the pad on the table and made a pot of tea. While she waited for it to brew, she walked around the table, looking at her work from every angle. Then she tore off the charcoal sheets and dropped them onto the floor.

She washed her hands and face and opened her grandmother's paintbox. The cubes had so little paint left that she had to grind the brush in circles to pick up enough pigment. She used the smallest brush and immediately realized her mistake. It took so long to paint an onion life-size. She started again with her largest brush, which would hardly fit into the cube but held much more paint. Soon she ran out of umber, then yellow ochre and both raw and burnt sienna. Late in the evening she realized that the onions were beginning to look pleasing because her eyesight was blurring. She rubbed her eyes and washed out the brushes, pushing the hairs down to release all paint. Then she shook them dry and stood them in an empty honey jar. The stove had long gone out.

The morning sky was empty of rain. The unfiltered light was cruel on her painting. The string of onions, so long separated from its nourishing clay, still retained an absolute life that gleamed like a gold snake. Her paintings were a flat, sterile shadow, marks upon a page; the pencil drawings an effortful study, painful, dull. Under her feet the charcoal smudges became more smudged. She picked up the sheets and turned them around. One sign, one forgotten impulse of her hand had made a shape that looked real, almost lively. One could imagine that the person who had made it had once seen an onion, perhaps.

She threw a woollen shawl about her shoulders and went out, stopping to hear the pebbles clink at the water's edge and to look at sea birds, riding the waves, their feathers packed tight against wet and cold. She admired them. She envied them. Effortless perfection. Walking back to the house she looked again and saw one rise slowly from the sea, driving itself up to where thermals carried it. Not effortless. Perfect through practice.

She stretched her arms and flapped her shawl-wings slowly, then fast, then in circles. She ran along the sand and leaped up. The birds rose together and wheeled away, shrieking. She leaped and ran, looking back at the deep gouges left by her boots.

At the house the open paintbox was almost empty. The jar of brushes stood guard. She found the charcoal sketch of an onion, tore it from the sheet and pinned it up on the dresser, then she bundled up all the other sheets and pushed them into the stove. She made porridge and, as she stirred, heard her night's labours crackle to hot dust. She finished the porridge, standing by the stove, eating from the pot, watching the day begin to change. The sky chilled. The sea went from blue to grey, an instant change as autumn asserted itself. She put an apple in her pocket, picked up her pad and box of charcoal and went in search of trees.

4

Geoff looked into the mirror on the cabinet door in the bathroom. It was the only mirror in the house. The furrows of his unshaven face were mildew grey, even the hair had a tarnished look. Dirty old man watching a naked woman rise from the waves. Venus indeed. A night of sticky loveless dreams. He went downstairs, put on the kettle and went to get milk from the fridge. He found the blackberries, their glass bowl frosted, a dull dew on the fruit. He put a berry in his mouth, tasting first a sweetness and then a bitterness, as though it had started to rot before becoming fully ripe. Or perhaps rain had killed it. He spat it out and tipped the blackberries into the bin.

The rain started at ten and by midmorning he had to turn on the lights in the shop. He sat behind the counter reading the paper and trying to concentrate. He tried to evoke the picture of Clare and Rosie but Clare's face was hidden by her hair and Rosie's face was without feature. Three years old, nearly four, like Stevie. Had she looked like Stevie? Twenty years of solid drinking had been too effective. Clare's face might come back. He could recreate the way she moved, the sound of her voice. He could describe her features: fair hair, blue eyes, fair skin: an identikit picture. Her face would not reveal itself and Simon, Simon as a child must have looked like Tom.

Tom, who looked so familiar. Familiar, familial. He rubbed his face. A drink. What wouldn't he give for a drink? Blot them all out. He stood up and went to the kitchen. The cat cried at the door and he let it in then rubbed it down with a towel. The cat settled in its basket near the radiator.

Customers strayed in to shelter from the rain. One or two browsed then bought. One stayed to talk: a regular. He was an American, planning a voyage through the canals of France. 'Wine tasting, really.' He winked at Geoff. He opened the maps of the regions and speculated about vineyards. 'Taste on the way down. Make our choices. Collect on the way back.' His dark green oilskins smelled faintly rancid. The raindrops that sat on his cap on the table soaked in, leaving dark circles on the wool. His voice was agreeable, deep and mellifluous. The room seemed almost to echo with his absence when, finally, he left. Geoff inhaled slowly and tried again to recreate Clare's face. Immediately, the woman from his dreams appeared, rising out of the water. He put down his mug and turned the pages of the paper but the haloed shape obliterated them. He went to the kitchen and opened the door to the garden. He breathed in the rain-heavy air and concentrated on naming everything he could see: grass, walls, shrubs, drops of rain. But then the glittering drops on her body: he started again. Grass, walls, shrubs, river. Sea water poured down between her breasts, a little river.

Grass, walls, shrubs: it was useless. He slammed the door and returned to the counter, pulling a book from a shelf as he passed. He opened it and read:

> *They never turn on me or you,*
> *prudent Peter,*
> *zealous Michael,*
> *enterprising Eve,*
> *Barbara, Clare.*

35

Clare. The coincidence must mean something, though he never believed in coincidences. Odd how when something is on your mind, references keep cropping up. He glanced at the rest of the poem.

> *If he ever owned anything, he has lost it*
> *and having lost it, doesn't want it back.*

Things, that must refer to. Lost things. Not people. Not love.

The swimmer threatened again and he dropped the book and picked up the paper noisily, then started to read at random, aloud. Just before the door opened, he saw through the glass a yellow shape moving and he stopped reading. A figure wearing waterproofs and wellingtons, an amorphous blob, hesitated on the threshold. He was so grateful for the distraction that he offered coffee and pointed out coat hooks. The figure lifted off its sou'wester and turned to hang it up, not noticing his stare. He put down the mug too fast and burned his hand. In the moment at which she turned, hearing him cry out, he retreated to the kitchen, where he ran cold water on his burnt hand. He glanced over his shoulder. He was not mistaken. The hair was now thick and fair but the shape of her neck, the curve of her jaw, her straight nose: there could be no doubt. A vision in PVC. That should calm him. It should make him laugh. Rescued not by the real but by the ridiculous. He put a spoon of coffee in a mug and showered grains on the draining board. He lit the gas, taking three matches to get the flame going. He wished she were gone and then turned to make sure she was not.

She moved slowly and calmly along the shelves, taking down a book here and there. He brought in the coffee and set it on the table near her and moved behind the counter, taking up the paper, gripping it tight to prevent his hand from shaking. He could not help glancing up and when he found her looking at him, he lowered the paper. Her eyes were grey or green, too deep-set for him to be sure. He attempted some chat that embarrassed him with its banality. Nonsense. He was talking nonsense. A girl in her late twenties, young enough to be his daughter, comes into the shop and he is sweating: senescence melting into gormless adolescence. She mentioned Inis Breac and he nodded like a puppet, an uncertain dislocated bob of the head that must have looked as though he was ducking something. She talked of swimming. Can she have seen him? Has she come in swaddled like Scott of the Antarctic (no, with her accent, Amundsen, more like) only to torment him? He wanted to vanish out the back door, to flee upstairs, anywhere. He wished she would go. She put something on the counter. 'I'll take this one,' she said. He wrapped the book while she wrapped herself, a crackling synthetic duet. 'Thank you for the coffee.' The door closed behind her.

He took off his glasses and held one hand over his eyes, clenching his forehead between fingers and thumb, aching from his sudden plunge into helpless youth.

He went to the telephone and pressed the digits of Becky's number. Simon and Becky's. He would welcome the sound of any voice but especially one from the centre of normality. The phone rang on. Simon would be in his workshop and Becky, but no, she would not be in the garden in this. The rain slipped sideways down the window in smooth, overlapping sheets. He dialled again. The phone rang out. They must have forgotten to put on the answering machine. He picked up the mug she had drunk from. It was still warm.

There were three pubs on the street. The green one at the end near the church, the brown one opposite it, and McCormick's, two doors away. From the corner of his eye, he knew its semi-circle of white letters glued to the window masking an interior the

37

colour of stout as it is poured, the diamond tiles of the entrance, cracked resting place for a collapsed labrador whose coat seemed several sizes too large, and the smell, the ancient fungal whiff. He released the catch on the door, turned the sign to 'closed', turned up his collar, then paused in the doorway's recess. Simon. Simon, Becky, Tom, Stevie. If he turned left, McCormick's would swallow him. With enough booze inside him, he wouldn't notice Simon's coldness, probably. Probably not. He turned right and rushed into Bective Antiques.

The lanky fellow perched on the edge of a table looked across the gilt picture-frame resting on his knee, the shaving brush still in one hand. A fine coat of dust made white patches on his corduroy trousers. Geoff stopped short. 'Mrs Thompson. Jenny?'

'Just a moment.' The young man put the frame down carefully and went through the curtain. Geoff caught sight of himself in an overmantel. The speckled glass showed an apparition. He turned down his collar and smoothed his hair. The room was warm. The furniture glowed. Each painting had a down light in a brass holder. One showed a convivial group with slouch hats, thigh boots, long pipes and rummers in their hands. The camaraderie of the shared glass: an alien concept. Books and an inkwell sat on a desk with an open ledger and some silver-framed photographs of women with hair piled softly, lace at their throats, before the improbable landscapes of the photographer's studio. He started to back towards the door and bumped into a low table. He heard footsteps coming swiftly from the interior. The curtain wafted aside and Jenny stood beaming at him. 'No need to say it,' she said. 'On a day like this, we all need cheering up. Tea?'

'Just what I need,' he lied, following her through the curtain.

'No more books for me?' she looked archly over her shoulder at him as he followed her upstairs.

''Fraid not.'

'Don't mind me, I'm just teasing. Olivia and I were getting tired of looking at one another. You'll be just the one to take us out of ourselves.'

Geoff glanced at the framed flower prints that mounted the stairs with him. No inspiration there. The stairs were broader than his, the house taller, three storeys. They were on the landing. No escape now. She opened the door to a large sitting-room. Olivia was in an armchair with a tartan rug on her knees, close to the fire whose redness traced the decorations in the cast-iron surround. A deep-bayed window hung with yellow curtains gave a summer brightness.

'Geoff has come to cheer us up,' said Jenny, 'and I'm just going to hurry Seán with the tea.' Geoff sat slowly down on the sofa. Resting his forearms on his knees, he clasped his hands and looked at Olivia. Her hair, face and hands all had the same glowing pallor.

'You're good to come.'

Geoff's hand moved towards his pocket, searching for his cigarettes. He reclasped his hands.

'I'm a refugee, really.'

'Really?' She closed the book that she had been holding.

'Not really, no.' He gestured vaguely. 'Just escaping.'

'The weather?'

'And everything.'

'Sometimes we go abroad at this time of year,' Olivia glanced towards the windows. 'But with the move and everything, we won't make it. Maybe after Christmas.' She looked too ill to move.

He nodded. 'That'll be nice.'

'We used to go. Just the two of us. Now we need Seán.'

'Yes,' said Geoff. Flowers in a bowl on a table in front of the fire quavered. Coal shifted and settled in the grate. He looked at her anxious smile. 'A winter holiday'd set you up. Somewhere warm. Somewhere,' he saw the heavy lid of the sky. 'Somewhere the swallows go back to?' His face reddened but she sat up.

'Exactly,' she said. 'Just that.'

Jenny came in carrying a brown teapot. Seán followed with a tray. Jenny put the teapot down on the table and moved the flowers. While Seán unloaded the tray, she gave out plates and sliced a fruitcake.

'You've met Seán, Olivia's boy. Mine are all abroad.'

'I'm abroad too, Jen,' said Seán.

'Yes, but not burrowed behind a desk somewhere. We hardly ever see them.'

She poured milk for Geoff. 'Seán is different,' she patted his arm.

'Nonsense. I only come back for the comfort. Nice fires. Lovely food. All that approval.' Seán settled next to Geoff and helped himself to milk. He smiled at Geoff. 'I'm only here for the pampering.' He put three lumps of sugar in his tea and stirred.

'You're always working. Helping out below. Running messages. I even have him cleaning frames now, did you see?' Jenny sat back on her heels, teapot in hand. Olivia looked from one to the other with pleasure, her tea and cake untouched.

They bantered on. Geoff and Olivia were silent, nodding or demurring when needed. Geoff, sunk in the velvet depths of the sofa, began to relax, hypnotized by the novelty of ease, the laziness of undemanding company. The strangeness of being assumed welcome, present without reservation, accepted without demand or test, kept him alert.

'We're forgetting our manners,' Jenny said, turning to him suddenly. 'Ignoring our visitor.' She offered cake. 'What about you? Tell us about yourself. I suppose you're like ourselves, fleeing the city.'

Geoff pushed himself upright. He looked at her kind face and wanted suddenly to catch that sense of connection that she took for granted.

'Well it was more that I'd always wanted to have a bookshop. Try it out anyway. And then my son and his family came over last June. Becky and himself wanted to bring their two lads up in the country. So they sold their house in London and bought a small holding. They'd seen this place on holiday. They were trying to find a ring fort on the Survey map and when they finally got there, there was this broken-down farmhouse with outhouses and all. Just perfect.' It was easy as long as he did not have to talk about himself.

'And they love it?'

'Yes.'

'And you too?'

'Me?'

'You're happy here too?'

In the silence of his hesitation they could hear the lid clink off the teapot as Jenny checked the tea. He shrugged. 'Oh, I don't care where I am. One small town is much the same as another.' He could sense their disappointment. He tried again. 'I mean, it's just handy for the family. For me, I mean. They came and I followed.' They nodded but Geoff's discomfort had silenced them.

Seán stood up. 'Make them tell you about themselves. They owe you now,' he said lightly. He took the teapot downstairs. Jenny put coal on the fire, crouching down and tilting the scuttle. When she had finished she paused, resting her forearm on one knee, watched the fuel start to catch fire and then turned towards Olivia.

'D'you remember our first visit? One of the things that appealed to us? Looking around the town, the little all of it, we noticed so many different accents, voices, even languages. It made the place seem festive, international and yet neighbourly. On first-name terms in the shops and with the locals.'

Olivia nodded. 'The place is so small. It suits us. We were each living alone,' she paused.

Jenny went on, 'You were used to that but I found it awful. So, we sold up and here we are.' She was talking to Olivia now, checking with her.

Olivia smiled at Geoff. 'We have the town, the sea , the country, all to hand.'

'We're near enough the city, the airport and so forth. And there are lots of us.' Jenny looked at him now.

'Sorry?'

'Settlers. Blow-ins. Not just in town. In the hinterland as well. Good for biz I'd say. And new suburbs, if that's the word for them. New bits on the edges. Prosperous-looking, anyway.' She put the tongs down and stood up. 'Funny how things change. This place used to be the tailor's. There was an old order book and cloth remnants, iron pins, would you believe, all rusted but sharp, and a shears, oh and buttons, a big tin of them.'

'We're thinking of giving the order book to the Heritage Centre,' said Olivia. 'The rest seem a bit sad. We don't know if they'd want them. It was quite a while since the house had been lived in.'

Geoff thought of the day he had spent clearing the shop and tried to remember what he had thrown out. The house had been empty of all but the kind of things that seem unwanted by anyone. Ubiquitous rubbish: torn cartons, a few knives without handles, a battered spoon, bits of newspaper. 'There was a strop, I think. A piece of hide, about this long.' He gestured. 'All mouldy. And basins. Enamel, all chipped.' A rotten piece of wood with some traces of white and red paint still lay in his back yard. He tried to make up for the lack of interest that had left him without small talk. 'Must've been a barber's.'

'Really?' Jenny was interested. 'And a few doors down there was a harness maker. We did wonder why it was that there were so many shop windows covered with net screens in this street.'

Seán returned with the replenished pot and poured more tea. Jenny held up her cup. 'What d'you think, Seán? Can this have been the tradesmen's quarter?'

'Isn't the café called 'The Old Shoemaker's'?'

'Then gradually all those old trades died out here, like everywhere.' Olivia looked thoughtfully towards the window and the fire crackled in the silence.

The shop bell rang.

'My turn.' Jenny hurried out of the room.

'That was a lovely book you brought,' said Olivia. 'You are interested in antiques?'

Geoff shook his head. 'I know nothing. Just found it in a box.'

'A pity.' Olivia looked across the room. 'There's a little chair there that was damaged on the way here. We're wondering where we can get it mended.'

The chair stood with its back to the wall, small and fragile, one of its curved legs broken.

'Simon,' Geoff said, 'he repairs furniture. My son.' The spell of the room broke. The yellow curtains were wan against the implacable dusk. 'I'll give you his number.' He fumbled in his pockets and found a biro under his cigarette packet. He could not find his notebook so he tore a piece off the packet and scribbled Simon's number. He glanced at the woman in the armchair, at her gentle candid gaze above the pleated lilac blouse and then at the ill-torn scrap of card. 'I'll ask him,' he said, 'it would be quicker,' and felt a small tug of dismay. Simon would not be pleased. He thrust the scrap into his pocket. Seán turned on all the lamps and closed the curtains.

'You'll stay to dinner, won't you? Jenny's orders.'

Geoff rose. 'I'd better go. Can't leave the shop too long. Thanks.' He made his goodbyes and was back at his own door while the antique shop bell still sounded.

The sky was clearing and people had reappeared on the street. Two customers followed him in and moved along the shelves, murmuring to one another. He went to the phone and while he pressed the numbers, felt in his pocket for his cigarettes. He could feel the broken edge of the packet when Simon answered. Simon was unenthusiastic. 'One chair? I'm very busy. Don't know when I'll have time.' Geoff edged a cigarette out of the packet with one hand. 'It's not very damaged. It might be just a matter of gluing it.' Simon sighed. 'Don't know when I'll get into town. Can't they bring it out?' Geoff could see him standing at the phone, turning to look out of the window, drawing his fingers through his hair, just like Clare used to. He could so nearly bring her face to mind but the effort of willing it to appear always caused it to vanish.

The man brought three books to the counter and the woman followed with two more. There were two old books of his among them. A brief lightness came over him as he put these remnants of his past into a bag and handed them over. They were a couple in their mid-thirties. He could not guess their occupation or origin. They sauntered off, closing the door without a sound.

Twenty past five. He went to the kitchen and lit the grill. The cat stirred in his basket and Geoff opened the back door. Catching a whiff of the river, the cat moved towards it, looked back towards the cooker, stood in the gap, tail curling speculatively, until there was a movement in the grass and then he was gone. Geoff shut the door and put two chops on the pan. He put a knife and fork on the table and took a plate from the draining board and put it on top of the grill. He went through the shop and turned the sign on the door and put on the catch. The smell of fat had begun to creep into the kitchen when he returned and he lifted the lever and pushed out the small top pane of the window. The meat started to spurt and hiss.

When he had eaten he put the leftovers on the cat's dish, set it on the doorstep and called into the dark. He heard only the faint slurp of the water in the overhanging grass and briars. He climbed the narrow curving stairs and turned on the television in the front room. Orange street light leached colour from the furniture. An unsteady trickle of cars was the only sound from outside. The febrile flutter of the screen was not interrupted by any ghost of living or dead. The only other movement in the room was of smoke, spiralling out to fill the air in uneven layers.

5

The shower started as Birgit threaded her way along the pavement towards the newsagents. The street emptied and she turned up her collar and walked faster but a broken gutter emptied a trail of heavy icy drops onto her face and she plunged into the nearest doorway. She could smell coffee and pastries and, without deciding, she found herself inside the café. She sat at a round table and ordered coffee. While she waited for the girl, she took out her pad and pen, rested her head on her hand and began to write.

'Your paintbox started something and I have been trying to capture whatever spirit or magic rose up when I opened the lid. I think I am in love with the materials the way a child is in love with the sand and the sea. I am trying so hard to mix the two – the water and the pigment – but it is like trying to make a house from smoke, except my efforts don't vanish, they are there to haunt me. Eventually I burn most of them, so they do vanish (as they should). But how are you? Any better? You must be better if you are home from hospital?'

Her coffee arrived, and as she laid down her pen and picked up the cup she saw a man smiling at her from a small table near the wall, where he was sitting by himself.

He stood up, tall and thin, and came to her table where he

rested one hand on the back of the chair opposite.

'You don't remember me,' he said. She shook her head.

'You are interested in painting.'

She stared at him.

'You were looking at the landscape in the antique shop. I was cleaning frames. A few days ago.' She nodded.

'May I?' He gestured towards a chair then paused, seeing her pad. 'But I'm interrupting.'

'No, no. It's hard. I'm not saying the right things. My grandmother is ill and I want to find something to say to cheer her but ...'

He had his head on one side and was gazing at her with polite sympathy. She closed the pad and cleared her throat.

'What was the painting?'

'Oh, just a landscape. After Poussin, I suppose you could say. Long after. I'm afraid it's sold.'

'Oh I didn't, I couldn't, I mean, I spend all my spare money on materials.'

He laughed. 'I'm not a salesman. I'm just helping my mother and aunt for a few days while I'm on leave.' He sat down and glanced at her hands, at her nails rimmed with blue. 'What d'you paint?'

She sighed. 'I don't paint. I battle with materials.'

'Oils?'

'Watercolour.'

He raised his eyebrows, 'Very difficult.'

She sat up suddenly. 'Are you a painter?'

'No, an architect, but I had some training. The basics.'

She looked at him, at his direct grey eyes, and made up her mind. 'Maybe you can tell me. I was going to buy more paint, more watercolours.'

'What about acrylic?'

'And abandon the other?'

'They'll be still there when you've finished exploring acrylic.'

The display stand at the stationers offered too much choice but Seán (she had learned his name on the way) pointed out the essentials and those, she found, used up all her money. She bought eight tubes: white, viridian green, ultramarine, cobalt, yellow, alizarin crimson, vermilion and yellow ochre. She could mix most of what she would need from those, he suggested. Below the racks of paints were trays of brushes. Seán chose three while Birgit paid for her paints and handed them to her outside the shop. She looked at the tightly rolled brown paper.

'Harder brushes,' he said.

A delivery van drove slowly up on the pavement and another shower started. Birgit took the parcel.

'I don't know what to say.'

'Don't say anything but let me come to Inis Breac. I'd like to see your work.'

'No,' she said, too abruptly, and then, 'it's not for show. But you can come. Come to visit the island,' she said, trying to make up for her rudeness. She pulled the edges of her coat together under her chin.

'I'm away again on Wednesday. Can I come tomorrow?'

She wanted to say no. Don't interrupt me. Take your too likeable eyes and thin face, your tangled hair and effortless ease away. Instead, she nodded and thanked him for the brushes.

'They weren't a bribe. They're essential.'

'Of course. You must come. I'll catch a fish.' She backed away. 'The ferry, the bus ...'

By Tuesday she had forgotten him.

It was like opening her grandmother's paintbox. She began with vermilion, then tried all the colours, pressing a blob of each onto an old enamel plate that she found at the back of the dresser. The new brushes had a spring and a resistance that spread the paint in pure colour. She covered every sheet of paper on both sides. The paper cockled and warped but she continued making larger and larger strokes. Some pages she covered in circles, others in rough streaks. She painted from the centre out and from the edges in. Every change of light showed something different or new. In the evening she switched on the single overhead bulb and worked in shadow, relishing the movement and turn of the brush even when she could not see clearly what was happening. She stuck a continuous line of sheets up on the walls and painted from one to the other, line upon line, until she was surrounded by colour, like a chinese dragon. When she ran out of paper, she pulled down the blind and painted lines from any poems she could remember, using the smallest brush. She painted panes of the window yellow, trying to eliminate all brush strokes and make an oblong of unblemished colour on the glass.

The following morning, when Seán knocked at the door, she did not hear him. He pushed it open and came slowly into the room. She was down to her last thread of ultramarine. She was seated at the table, her hands and clothes splattered with multi-coloured paint; before her, her empty writing pad, whose leaves were covered with shapes that might have been birds. Jars of dark grey liquid jostled with mugs of cold coffee. The enamel plate was a congealed palette and the walls of the room a manic dance of colour. She looked at him, mystified. He started to laugh. He rocked back and forth, shaking his head.

'Shy,' he spluttered. 'Oh, please!' He pulled out a chair and slumped into it, dropping his parcels on the floor. 'I thought, I thought ...' he shook with another spasm. 'I thought you were shy about your painting!' he gasped. She stared at him. 'How were you going to hide this lot? And why?' The yellow panes caught his eye and he roared again.

She sat up. 'Why would I want you to see this?' she demanded. 'Why? Because it's not painting.'

'Oh, I don't know.' He wiped his eyes. 'It's like something that a whirling dervish would make.'

She looked around the room. She had been so engrossed in her experiments that she had not looked at their cumulative effect. It was as if some centrifugal force had been set off. Seán glanced up to the white lampshade on which she had painted orange stars. He started to laugh again then caught her eye. She stared at him then said, 'Well I didn't touch the ceiling.' Then they both laughed.

She stood up and moved mugs and jars to the sink. They cleared the table. She set the kettle on the stove and bundled up all the loose sheets that were lying around. When she started to pull down the paper from the walls, he stopped her. 'The day's so dark,' he said.

She went to the window and looked out for the first time that day. Grey sky, grey sea. She turned to him. 'Perfect weather for fishing. And I forgot! I promised!' She took down the rod from the beam and they left the house.

They climbed down the rocks and sat on an uneven ledge. He watched as she cast her line neatly, then waited, very still. Only fair strands of her hair moved in the intermittent breeze. The horizon was hardly visible, a stage at which dark grey began to change to pale grey. Two trawlers floated silently in the distance.

'There,' she whispered.

He looked down and saw something pale under the water, like

a strip of paper fluttering. Then in one sudden whirl, she landed a fish. She unhooked it and, putting her thumb in its mouth, jerked the head backwards. The fish was still. A seagull wheeled over them then dropped into the water and approached slowly. Birgit took a knife from her pocket and cut off the fish's head. Then she gutted it and threw the maroon jelly of entrails to the gull. More gulls moved in. She washed her hands and the knife. She did not look at him until she had finished. He had a sense that she was alone, at ease with the rocks and the sea.

'What d'you think? Shall we eat it?' she said suddenly, over her shoulder, from where she crouched on the waterline.

'Taste all right?'

'Mm. Pleasant. Easy to catch. Easy to kill. No resistance, so it's not exciting to eat. But fresh.' She put out her hand and he pulled her up.

They boiled it in sea water, the same water that the potatoes had been cooked in and then finally, two large handfuls of sea kale. Birgit put the food out and handed Seán a plate. 'You must eat quick. The plates are cold.'

When he had finished he said, 'That was very good.'

'Very simple,' she said. 'But you can see,' she got up to make tea, 'I do not live in luxury. I cook and keep house as little as possible. Not a bit like an architect, or not like the architects I know. They have perfect apartments full of clean lines and they have very high standards in food too. Are you like that?'

'I don't have an apartment or a home, yet anyway. I stay with my mother when I'm here and the rest of the time I'm on the move. Following the work, going where I'm sent.'

'Where is that?'

'Africa. Different countries, building whatever is needed. Clinics mainly, I do contract work with a variety of agencies. It is a far cry from the kind of life I'd have here.'

51

'Why have you chosen this?'

'A friend and I took a year off after school, worked on building sites in England for a bit then bought a motorbike and set off down through France. In every town we stopped we'd take bets on the cathedral or the church: how long it took to build, how many years to finish. Then we crashed the bike: a disagreement with a cow in the Pyrenees. The cow won, the bike lost and we carried on hitching down through Spain.'

He clasped his hands behind his head and sighed comfortably.

'I think it was the best year of my life. Nothing prepares you for Spain. Or me anyway. Sitting in a rooftop café overlooking Barcelona with the sun setting? We ran out of money, of course, but we worked at anything and everything: bars, grape-picking, cleaning offices. It was all a lot of fun We were in love with a couple of Spanish girls.'

Birgit smiled and he shrugged.

'To be honest, we fancied all Spanish girls but these two took pity on us.' He stopped for a moment then continued. 'We were having a picnic out the country one Sunday and we saw this castle, a sort of fort, perched on a mountain, away in the distance. It was like a mirage but dusty, gaunt, even in that shimmering heat. We'd seen Moorish buildings before but close up: all grace and colour with those patterned tiles and little courtyards and so on, but this was a monster. It was ...' He glanced at the paintings.

'It can't have been colourless. I suppose it was ochre, like sand, something quite inhuman. Gordon kept staring at it and afterwards he said he just had to see what sort of people built it.' He gave a faint laugh. 'I'm not sure he ever found them.'

'So you went to Africa?'

'Yeah. Morocco and on down over the Atlas Mountains. We stayed for a couple of weeks and then our money ran out again and there was no work and we came back. But that was it for

Gordon. He didn't find his Moorish invaders but he'd seen the wealth and the poverty and he wanted to ... well, he was very driven. He signed up for Voluntary Services and vanished overseas.'

'But not you?'

'Oh I'm more cautious. And I think my mother had had her fill of anxiety by then so I came back. Went to college and when I finished got a job and a nice flat overlooking a river, spent my days designing fancy lighting systems, spiral staircases, conservatories. It was a lot of fun.'

'For poor harassed executives in need of meditation space?'

He grinned. 'Especially if the lifestyle mags say so.'

'How did you come to change?'

'It was Gordon, mainly. He kept in touch. The contrast between his work and mine, his life and mine, intrigued me. At the end of a day I'd be happy at having convinced a client that brushed steel was a better finish than chrome for kitchen taps, and he'd have dug a well. All that agonizing over colour charts. After a while it can come to seem trivial.'

'You could have changed your job. Aren't there other things?'

'Mmm. I did try working on a housing scheme: doing a layout for gardens, playgrounds, sports facilities, community centre, the lot, and then the government changed and the budget was cut and the end was ...' He frowned and clenched his fingers around the mug. 'It was a travesty. A monument to meanness.'

'That was hard.'

'It seemed such a lost opportunity.' His face darkened and she waited for a moment.

'And then after that, what did you do?'

'Handed in my notice. Took a few days off and looked at my life. I was coming up to thirty. I had no ties.' He saw her look of puzzlement. 'No girl. No lovely Spanish Lady to take pity on me, so I signed up with an aid agency and I go wherever I'm sent.

There was no great blinding flash of inspiration, I just had a gradual realization that I was resisting the obvious.' She seemed to be waiting for something. 'Have you never been too comfortable to move?'

She ignored the question and behind it a disconcerting image of Peter, his chin multiplied in layers that that overlapped. 'This "obvious". What was it?'

'To make a practical contribution: sink a well, install a pump, build a school, whatever.' He made a face. 'I'm beginning to sound like a convert.'

'No. Tell me.'

'The first place we went, the first village, their health was so bad, babies always sick, food contaminated. And then when they got the well: it was no miracle, just one small change that broke the cycle.'

'Life was transformed for those people?'

'It went from being impossible to tolerable.' He swilled the forgotten tea around in its mug.

Birgit took it from him and threw the dregs down the sink. She filled it with fresh tea and sat down again.

'This is a silly question, I think but I should like to know, are you happy?'

'Happy?' He sounded vague, as though he had forgotten the meaning of the word. 'While I'm there, yes. But holidays are ... are unsettling. Other thoughts, other lives. My mother isn't getting any younger. Her health. I don't know.' He shook himself and sat up. 'But what about you?'

'Me?' She gestured about her. 'It is what you see. I try to paint. I fail. I try again.'

'For how long?'

She laughed. 'That bad, eh?'

He started to protest.

54

'No. I know what you mean. I've been here since midsummer. I made a – what is it called – a leave of absence? From my job, my work.' His sudden attention had flustered her and her English faltered. 'I was, am, a teacher.' The recollection steadied her. 'Of small children. The children of diplomats and international businessmen. For five years. And then –'

'And then?'

'After five years we can take a year off. Unpaid, of course, but I had saved. So I took a bus, a plane, a train, another bus and a boat. Then I walked. I just wanted to get away, as far as I ever could.'

'From small children?' He raised one eyebrow..

'Oh, they are fine. Spoiled but, their parents: less loveable. No, it was Peter, my – what do they say in England? My "old man".'

In the silence she looked at the grain of the table and scraped it with her thumbnail. 'We had been together since I was sixteen and we were ... our life was too ... too finished. Not ended, no, but, what's that silly word? Comfy? Like a pair of old cushions.'

Seán's voice was mild. 'Nothing wrong with comfort.'

'At twenty-five? Perhaps when I am fifty I will be glad of it and when I am seventy, then I may need it. But no. Oma, my grandmother: she's seventy-four and she lives alone on the top floor – she will not use the lift. She puts her shopping in, so the fantastically proper people who live in the other apartments have to travel with apples and fish and birdseed while Oma climbs the stairs. That is how I'd like to be.'

He watched her, his face softening as she spoke.

'So you are. Not quite seventy-four – yet – but independent. You live alone –' he glanced around.

'You look as though you are waiting for someone to leap out of a cupboard!'

He cleared his throat. 'Just checking.' Shaking his head he added, 'Aren't you lonely? On my way here I met no one, not a soul. Don't you ever miss your friends, family?'

'In the summer it was busy, my parents visited, but I have not time to be lonely. I am used to occupying myself. My father is a teacher, my mother is a psychologist: they have busy lives and I have no brothers or sisters. I am used to occupying myself.'

'Ah. I'm an only child too.'

'So you understand.'

He looked around at the walls. 'The only child comes to the edge of the world and spends all her time painting.'

'Does that seem strange? You have made a change that is just as great.'

'I'm never alone. And when I'm there, in Africa, I feel absolutely at the centre.'

She gazed at him, hearing the unforced certainty in his voice and trying to imagine his life.

He shook his head again slowly. 'I could never be this self-sufficient.'

'No?'

'Relying all the time on inner resources? Too hard.'

'Hard! From the kind of life I had, with every moment of my time mapped out, this to me is luxury.'

The room darkened and small knotted clouds threatened blustery winds and showers. At the same moment they became aware of the clock on the dresser, of its disinterested ticking.

'Should I?' He turned to look out of the window.

'The crossing could become very uncomfortable.' She got up and reached for their coats.

The wet sand hardly yielded to their footsteps as they crossed the first beach, its surface studded with the small change of the last tide. He picked up an orange shell.

'These would be used as decorations, around the doors of the houses.'

'Shells?'

'Too far from any sea but little, pretty things. Bits of broken crockery.'

Still walking, Birgit picked up a handful and sorted it to keep only the perfect ones. They climbed the rocky arm of land that separated the first beach from the second and she bent at a pool to wash the sand from them and shook them in her cupped hands to drain off the water. He watched it trickle through her fingers and glanced around.

'Where d'you get fresh water?'

'There are springs and streams. There's no shortage, even in summer.'

She handed him the shells and he looked at the hard perfect curves and angles for a moment before putting them in his pocket, where they ground gently together and dried slowly in the warmth, leaving the salt tacky on his hand. They were on the road leading to the pier. Their coats whipped and flew about their legs in the cold unsteady wind. He looked at her, ready to thank her, but she had her head down and was frowning at the pools on the road. Then she turned to him.

'Where do you get water? The well?'

'Not enough there for building. Four miles we have to go to find it. The water hole gets very low at some times of year. The women walk every day, all day, backwards and forwards, just for cooking.'

'And for building?'

'For building a clinic, the whole village walks, even the men.' He looked at her, smiling. 'Oh, yes. Carrying water is not a man's job. This is a big concession.'

'D'you carry water?'

He straightened his back and eased his shoulders. 'And how. You become an ox. You feel strange without a yoke. At the start you get blood blisters on your shoulders. But soon,' he shrugged, 'you become an ox.'

She stared, appalled.

He smiled. 'It's not a death sentence, not even a life sentence, for me.'

'How long will it be?'

'To complete? A couple of months. And then there will be a party for the whole village. Every woman, child, man.'

She leaned her head to one side. 'You put the men last.'

He laughed. 'They are the first with the ideas, they say.'

'And you?'

'No different, I'm afraid. Until I had to be.' He made a conscious melodramatic sweep. 'I laid down my pen and took up the bucket.'

They had arrived at the pier. The ferry bucked and plunged on the sharpening waves.

'So much water and all going to waste, tch!'

They laughed and then he stayed silent, looking at the sea.

'You love your work,' she said.

He looked from her hair that followed the line of her head and neck, then looked down to her hands and up to her face.

'I forget that there is anything else.'

The ferry docked. The ferryman threw a blue rope around the bollard at the bow and tied an orange rope through an iron ring at the stern. He heaved the grey bags ashore and started up the road to the post office.

'I thought there would be more time,' said Birgit, 'but here is my neighbour.' She introduced Seán to an elderly woman who climbed aboard the ferry, nimbly avoiding hazards to her high-heeled shoes and good coat. Margaret made jesting small talk until the ferryman returned. Birgit helped him cast off and Seán climbed into the boat. Then, still standing, he held out his hand and looking up at her said, 'Look under the table. That's the best help I can give.'

The boat's engine thudded and he let go of her hand.

Dear Oma,

I had my first visitor yesterday. He left me a big parcel of paints and today I have bought more paper and board. My efforts made him laugh. The room looked like an explosion, I suppose. I don't know. I was in the centre, having such a wonderful time. And he thought my life hard! But still, I produce nothing, except perhaps a small sketch of a hedge which I will send to you. It is in charcoal. I went out to find trees but there are so few on this island. So I made sketches of hedges, mostly without leaves. They look like crooked bones. The box says this charcoal is made from wood. How strange, to chop down a tree, burn it, put the pieces in boxes to be bought by someone to make drawings of trees. Should I take the ashes of my work and scatter them at the base of the hedges as an offering? Then one day, who knows, maybe branches of the hedge will be made into charcoal. The hedges here are all blown to one side, or they grow on one side only. Sometimes they look as if they are reaching out, sometimes crouching down. They need a kind God, the God of gentle breezes, perhaps. When the wind comes over the sea from the north-west, it is easy to imagine how they feel. I stay close to my stove and write.

I could send you a postcard of false turquoise skies but you would not believe it. You will believe my charcoal hedge, with all its faults, because it is real. I will go to the post office now.

As she lifted down her waterproof from its hook, there was a loud knocking at the door and it was pushed open. Red-faced, Margaret stood on the doorstep beside a wheelbarrow on which were heaped a gas drum, a bag of coal, two bags of groceries and a box. She tugged the box, long and bulky, from the pile and bore it across the threshold, like a trophy folded in her arms. She left it down on the table and stood back panting.

'This is for you,' she said, smiling at Birgit between gasps. Birgit pulled out a chair and Margaret sat down.

'You brought this all the way from the post office? You will have tea. You must, after such a journey.'

Margaret nodded, still trying to catch her breath. Her vivid eyes looked huge in a small triangular face. Her feet hardly reached the floor. A child's wonder looked out from her old face.

'He didn't want me to have it,' she said of the postmaster. 'He would have you go for it. He wouldn't be responsible.' She nodded. 'But I told him and the others backed me.'

Birgit could see the little room with the handful of old men discussing her parcel. The postmaster would advise caution. There would be more arguments. The jurors, reckless in their righteousness, would declare that a big parcel like that would have to be transported by wheelbarrow anyway, so Margaret's presence would be nothing less than the providence of God. Birgit promised to reassure the postmaster immediately. Margaret's breathing slowed and she looked around the room. Her eyes widened and she swivelled in her chair.

'You like the bright colours so,' she said, following the line of painted sheets around the walls. 'They said that you were an artist.'

'A painter is what I would like to be, but I am a beginner.'

Margaret's eyes glanced past her again to the walls. 'You'd need a lot of paint so. Or maybe equipment.' She did not look at the box.

'Yes, maybe.' Birgit took a scissors from the drawer of the table. 'Maybe this is something. Shall we see?'

Margaret nodded, speechless with polite curiosity.

The scissors was ineffective against the brown adhesive tape. Seeing its resistance, Margaret suddenly attacked the parcel with her hard broad hands and wrenched the cover back to show a box which was an easy victim. She pushed it towards Birgit. 'You can open it now,' she said and then, as Birgit took off the lid, she stared at the jumble of metal wires and springs.

'What would they be?'

'Lamps! Anglepoise!' Each had a long flex, to reach to the single socket, and there was an adaptor. A note folded inside the box read, 'As the days get shorter, these may come in useful. See you at Christmas, S.'

'From Seán,' she said, smiling down at Margaret's upturned face. 'To help me see in the dark! You met him on the ferry.'

'Well I remember him. We had a grand chat all the way in, in the bus after.' Margaret was happy with the connection. 'And he sends you lamps.' She watched as Birgit finished assembling and switched on the white-shaded lights.

'So I can see my mistakes,' said Birgit, patting her on the shoulder. 'I'll practise all winter and then in the spring.'

'You'll be ready for the scenery!'

'And I can use them around the house as well.'

Margaret looked approving. The lamps had become a proper present.

'He's a thoughtful person,' she said.

They looked at the shining white lines and curves. The shades cast down a warmth as well as light. 'And there's no shortage of scenery.'

'Inis Breac is beautiful,' said Birgit.

'And Oileán Cré, now wait 'til you see that. That's Jerome's home place. We visit it regular. Oh you'll have to see Oileán Cré.'

They drank their tea. Margaret looked around the room. 'You haven't changed it much,' she said. ''Twas Molly Bohane's house. Molly and me were at school together and friends always. She'd be glad to see you like the place as she had it.' She finished her tea and stood up. She would not have more, she had two long hills to climb before she reached home and there was a bag of groceries to be delivered to her neighbour. She was loud in her refusal of help but Birgit put on her coat and opened the door to where the wheelbarrow stood waiting. They took turns, with the wind dragging and chafing their clothes.

She unhooked the string of onions and placed it under the lamps. In the light, the onions shed their cocoon of brown and had become gold charged with pink, red and orange. She poured a large jar of water and laid out the colours in graded rows from pale yellow to darkest blue. She chose a big brush and started to paint.

The yellow windowpanes became more prominent as the

unpainted ones receded into the dark and wood in the stove subsided in muffled spasms, unnoticed. Birgit saw only the paint and the onions' gilded curves. At last a moth, singed by a bulb, fell onto the board and she had to pick it out, carefully lifting its legs from the liquid paint. When she opened the door to put it out, the cold and dark hit her as one force. She poked at the stove, found no spark and, yawning, turned off the lamps. The after-image of the onions dazzled her as she stumbled towards the bedroom.

6

Simon's workshop was spread through three sheds that descended on a slope at right angles to the house. Empty of cattle, hay and potatoes, they had been newly whitewashed and the windows and doors painted red, to match those of the house. The old slates, thinning and rounded at the corners, had been repaired and the ridge tiles renewed. The tiny windows had been cleaned almost to invisibility and the light they gave softened the unblinking glare of several fluorescent strips that ran down the apex of the unlined roof.

Geoff climbed out of the passenger seat and took the broken chair from the back of the car, while Olivia opened the gate. He had to stop himself from rushing to open it, just as he had had to stop himself from watching her drive. He had not yet got used to this revitalization, this island of vigour that lay in the flow of her illness. She seemed to have grown taller. Over the previous weeks her colour and her voice had strengthened. He realized one day, as she stood in his shop turning the pages of a book on Italy, that she was younger than Jenny.

She had seemed so low at Seán's departure. Geoff had been unable to refuse Jenny's request that he visit her often. He had hesitated at first and then one day he had come across a book of Chinese watercolours on the Yang-tse River. It followed the path

of the river over more than a hundred pages, the gorges, mountains and valleys; the towns on its banks; bridges, boats and fishermen, traders and travellers, moments from history, battles,
raids and pirates, and, through all, the powerful curling waves,
winding like a dragon's tail.

Olivia loved the book. She turned the pages backwards and
forwards, scrutinizing, comparing. It was very large and heavy.
She gave it a permanent place on a table in the bay window of the
sitting-room.

'It is better than a film,' she said one day to Geoff. 'You can go
back and you can stop. And on days like this,' she gestured
towards the window where the weather had set everything in a
motionless fog, eliminating the hills and the trees and gelatiniz-
ing the river, 'it brings life, somehow.' She returned to leafing
through the book.

'It might be to do with the lack of words, but I find I can bury
myself in the pictures.'

He wondered what it would be like to be so gripped by the
imagery of the illustrations that a very ill woman could use the
word 'bury'. Perhaps it had no meaning, or she did not hear it,
just as he had been able to look at the illustrations of the river
without any of the uneasiness he felt when close to water.

'And d'you know, I've looked at it so much that I've begun to
invent stories about the people in it? Some of them remind me of
people I know. There's a musician here ...' Her voice began to
quaver. She glanced at Geoff. The book was the thing offered,
not an exchange of daydreams. 'I suppose it's a bit fanciful but it
keeps me amused.'

He leaned against the window frame, light falling on one side
of his face.

The fog had paralysed the air above the river and between
them. Footsteps on the stairs made him frown. Not now, he

thought, leaning his forehead against the pane to receive its small dull shock that might bring some thought, some commonplace inspiration for him to offer to the sad still woman behind him.

'Music,' he blurted, as Jenny opened the door. She was halfway across the room, carrying a feather-duster.

'Sorry?'

'We were talking about music.'

'How the human voice is an instrument that cannot bear the weight of too much emotion,' said Olivia.

Geoff and Jenny looked at her. Jenny stopped.

'Well that doesn't sound very cheerful, but,' she diverted to a shelf beside the fireplace. 'The CDs are all here.'

'We were just looking at the book.'

'Oh, that.' Jenny's smile radiated towards them. 'That marvellous book.' She paused beside Olivia and glanced down. 'Mm. I hadn't noticed that picture. But d'you know my favourite?' She flapped over the pages. 'Here.'

Geoff and Olivia relaxed towards her.

'Here. See? That's us.'

Two middle-aged women sat under a tree, eating cherries and, it seemed, laughing.

'That's us. Not exactly merry widows but not so unmerry either.' She glanced at Geoff. 'And of course, we're luckier.' She straightened up. 'What did I come to say? Oh, yes. Tch. My head.' She twitched the duster. 'Feather-brained. There's a man, a customer.' She nodded towards the stairs.

'For me?' Geoff waited.

'You must go and see to him.' Olivia's voice was quiet.

Jenny stood holding the door open.

He had opened the bookshop as a matter of habit, though by

October most of the holiday-makers were gone and it would be November before the Christmas sales began: he wanted to show Becky that he was occupied. She called in when she brought vegetables to the shops or to the Country Market but he had not visited her and Simon since the day at Inis Breac. Occasionally, she brought the boys in and they sat at the centre table turning the pages of books, or played in the garden with Dundee while Geoff and Becky drank coffee. He kept orange juice in the fridge and crayons and paper on a shelf. He gave them each a new book when they were going home.

He had not seen nor spoken to Simon and now, as he watched Olivia stepping jauntily ahead of him down the smooth pink sandstone flag steps, he held the chair before him, part offering, part shield.

She tapped on the door and opened it. The passageway was cramped with furniture in transit. Finished pieces wrapped in cling-film gleamed beside the bruised and tattered row of newcomers. Simon was surrounded by chairs and sofas, stools, tables and couches. Bolts of fabric stood against the walls and in the corners. Clusters of springs were suspended from the ceiling like spiders above coils of herringbone webbing, tins of varnish and wax, and chunks of wood. Behind Simon was a sewing machine and in front of him, on a rough table, a rosewood chair partly covered in dark green fabric.

Olivia introduced herself and waved her hand: 'Geoff's helping.'

Simon looked at her and then at the chair. 'Best put it on the table then.' He moved a box of tacks and a book of samples. Geoff put the chair on the table and stood back. Simon ran his hands over it. 'Dainty,' he said and looked at the broken leg. He touched the long split.

'It's one of a set,' Olivia said, 'we'd really love to get it fixed.'

Simon peered at the joint between the leg and frame. 'Did you know it had worm?' He examined the whole chair closely. 'Only here, fortunately, but the leg'll need replacing.'

'And you are so busy.' Olivia was apologetic

'Oh, it's a nice piece of work. Very.' He set the chair gently on the workbench and patted it. 'I'll have to turn a new leg and gild it. Not a run-of-the-mill job: so fine. It'll be a treat.' He jerked his head towards the ranks of solid sofas and armchairs. 'I'll have to clear the decks. That'll take a few weeks.'

Olivia began to thank him. He smiled at her. 'It's no bother. As long as you're not in a hurry. Christmas be all right?'

'Wonderful.'

'I'd offer tea but Becky's not here and I am, as you see ...'

'Up to your eyes,' said Olivia.

He came with them as far as the gate, talking to Olivia about his latest commission. He held the car door open for her and as she sat in, he looked across the roof towards Geoff. 'Becky says you're coming for Christmas.' Geoff paused in the open door.

'I don't know.' He glanced away.

'Her orders. Nothing you can do.' Simon bent to look in at Olivia. 'I'll give you a ring.'

They were silent as they passed bare beech trees, branches metallic against the pale sky.

'He's handsome, your Simon.'

'He ... uh ... he takes after his mother.'

'Really? I would have thought,' she looked at him and then looked quickly back at the road. After a moment she said, 'You can smoke, you know. I don't mind. I was a smoker once.'

He took out his cigarettes, opened the window a couple of inches and lit up.

'I don't want to interfere,' she said, 'but you're very welcome to come to us for Christmas. We're hoping Seán will be home.

Don't say anything now.'

'You are very kind.' He wanted to tell her that kindness was unbearable, that the casual coldness of his son was more tolerable. He smoked and looked out of the side window. A hedge, a tree, a road-sign: props that prompted his recovery. Things to name while his heartbeat slowed and the tense knot in his head unravelled and sank.

'I must tell you,' she said. 'There were times when Seán and I didn't talk to one another. Two years, on one occasion. I had this dread, you see, of him being a mammy's boy, after his father died. So I pushed him away and when he was seventeen, he took off around the world. It was eight months before I even had a card. I'd trained him too well for independence. He came back, of course. And I'd learned to believe that he would survive. Now he comes back because he wants to.'

'If only it was up to me,' he said.

In the bookshop the air was stale. The central heating dried it and intensified the cigarette smoke. He opened the back door and fed the cat, putting scraps on a plate and watching while each one was lifted carefully and eaten, a few inches away from the doorstep, eyes fixed on the rest of the food. He walked down to the river and saw it move, swift and silent, barely picking up light.

Then an image came to him: he was beside a fire with a small child on his knee, reading a book. The child's gaze left his face only when a page was turned. Simon was sucking his thumb and stroking his nose with his forefinger. Geoff stepped back from the edge of the river and went up to the house. Dundee moved aside from his quick tread. He lit the fire in the sitting-room, fanning it to make it catch. When the rain-damp kindling had made a small heart of flame, he went downstairs and picked out a children's book about a train. Why not? It was old enough, it might have been the one, and pulling an armchair up to the fire, he sat down with the book open on his knee. Then he held the book in his left hand and crooked his right arm on the arm of the chair. He started to read aloud. His voice sounded false in the empty room. He lowered it and turned his head towards the book and read with his eyes half closed. That was how it must have been. Between bath and bed. The child, his child, in pyjamas, the hitched-up legs showing thin white calves, slippers tilting on the toes. One leg swinging. The slipper falling off, the child still gazing up at his face.

He read on. The story called for gruff voices, funny voices. He faltered. It was hopeless. Nothing in the book was familiar. The child could have been any child with any parent, anywhere: Simon with Stevie on his knee at this moment.

He closed the book. The willed image had become faint with effort. Best let it go.

The phone rang, a welcome interruption, now. It was Becky.

'Simon said you'd come with a very pretty woman, the owner of the antique shop? A business partner?' Geoff was not sure. As usual he was lame in the easy commerce of gossip.

'But you will come for Christmas, won't you? It's all arranged. The boys are really pleased.' Request, assumption, reaction, all in one urgent sentence. Only a curmudgeon would hesitate.

'Of course, yes. Yes, I'll come.'

'Oh, that's wonderful. I'll tell them.'

So she hadn't told them. She must be afraid too. He felt a chill that got colder as she chattered on.

'If there's any bother about it,' he intervened.

'No, no. There won't be.'

'If there's any bother,' he persisted, 'you mustn't worry. No really, I mean it. I've been invited next door.' She would not hear of it. He should just have refused. He should have told her that he had already accepted. Now it was too late. As he hung up the receiver, he wondered if he were a diplomat or a coward. The sounds of a band came faintly from the Town Hall.

7

Dear Oma,

When I got your card at the post office, I made such an exclamation that the postmaster and his friends assumed that I had heard from 'the boyfriend'. All my post, if you were to believe them, comes from some deserted lover. It is so good to know you are better again. I can see you, lying on the day bed with your wool stole around your shoulders, writing with the tortoiseshell pen that Granddad had during the war. When I was small, I used to touch the engraving and wonder what 'RN' meant. Did I ask you? I remember being very puzzled as to how his pen returned from the sea but he did not. In the end, I imagined that you had found it: gone down to the water's edge and searched and searched until, among a tangle of seaweed, you caught its mother-of-pearl gleam.

I walk along the seashore every day and find only flotsam: wood, shells, weeds of all sizes and colours from almost black to brilliant pink; sea urchins, bristles gone, just a wafer-thin hollow gourd with a pin-pricked pattern that the islanders say is the image of the Virgin Mary. And stones. Stones, stones, stones. Once I thought that all stones were grey but now, every stone is different and there are more colours than I can make on my palette, my enamel plate.

The weather has been so wet. I have spent weeks indoors, though I try to go out at least once every day. I have painted my dwindling string of onions as if to preserve them were my life's work. And then I eat them, making soup. Why do I bother to paint them so much? They are easy. Their colours are easy to blend. Their almost-roundness is not difficult, at that size. Most of all, they love the light. The specks of gold on their skin make them glow under the lamps. Was it you who told me that Marilyn Monroe had fine gold hairs on her face which caught the flash from the cameras and gave her a unique illumination? I paint and eat onions but I do not dream of them and I do not burn everything I paint. I have to face my mistakes, yes, but that means that I am less likely to repeat them. Often I don't recognize them immediately but when I go back again, more are revealed. It could be depressing but sometimes I think I see improvement. I have attempted almost everything in the house: chairs (very difficult), the table alone. The table, dishes and books; bowls, jugs, shells: what are called 'still life', but they are anything but still. Fruit rots, flowers fade (not that there are many now), fish lose their colours very fast, so I have to paint very fast. Chairs and tables and crockery are more 'still', but they are made of contours, lines, move-

73

ment, which can change very much with the light or the angle from which I approach them. It is strange, as the weather roves around the house, looking for ways to enter, while here inside, I am (more silently) pacing, watching, trying to gain entry to the secret life of things. It seems sometimes that I am learning not to paint or draw but to look. Perhaps that means I have become a bit more used to the materials. Though each time I uncap a tube of paint and see the colour fresh upon the enamel, it gives me pleasure, now there is also anticipation of what that colour might lead to.

You would not be so unkind as to tell me that I could learn all this from a course at the Polytechnic. (Mother has sent me a book but if I follow its instructions I will paint like the author and that seems to me a waste of time – I should then have to start again.) In some ways a college course is appealing (the camaraderie), but I think I am past my student days. Perhaps it is just selfishness but I want to try to grind out my understanding as people used to grind out paint, sifting precious colours from rocks, earth, plants. You will laugh, but I think you will understand. I have had my formal education. All those years of English and teaching were enough. Now I go back to the beginning, to kindergarten. I was so methodical, so 'good'. You should see this room! I do no housework, or just enough. I wash dishes once a day. I clean out the stove when it gets choked. I tie my clothes to the branch of a hedge that overhangs a little stream up the hill. This happens once a week or maybe less. But I keep my brushes clean and my paints in military rows. The paper and the board are stored flat under two big books on my bedroom floor. So there is order and, I hope, progress.

Some things I cannot paint at all. One is a mask that Seán has sent me. It hangs on the wall, though not where I paint, as it has too much presence, or it reproaches me with my inability to draw. It is of some hardwood, perhaps ebony, with heavy lips and closed eyes. The skull rises to a point and there are two rows of inlaid stone, something green, like a necklace but on the forehead, a mosaic, so simple but so fine. It is highly polished and has a 'dark' smell, if that means anything. It is the essence of the strange closed face. Seán says that there are many such, all with the same withdrawn look. I would say, in a whimsical way, that it does not want to be painted, but it does not seem to have any wants. And yet it is not inhuman. It is warm and marvellous to touch. But it is finished. To do more (try to paint it) would be to make a bad copy, I think.

Seán sends cards occasionally but do not worry. I am not going to repeat my mistake with Peter. I may have burned his letters but I do not forget how the weight of his certainties made me feel. I almost drowned in them. If you can write again, please do.

8

On Christmas Eve Geoff closed the bookshop at four, when the throng of last-minute buyers had thinned out. He opened the back door and looked out across the frosty grass to the river, which was motionless in the remains of the sunset. He called to the cat and waited, then put a plate of food near the doorstep and closed the door. He took two books from under the counter, one on the towns of northern Italy for Olivia and one on eighteenth-century houses, for Jenny. He could imagine their reactions: polite and warm to his polite and unimaginative offerings. The white Christmas lights that he had hung on the ceiling, made a tiny fairyland glow as he considered the books. He had never been good old reliable Geoff, why start now? His imagination, which had tried to build on the glimpses of his wife and daughter that came unexpectedly, on seeing the hand of a child resting on the counter or hearing the laughter of a stranger passing in the street, refused to be ordered and would not yield to any system-atic approach. But Christmas presents surely could not be beyond it.

He would not take a look in the mirror and risk discovering that that tattered map might have begun to show something of acceptance, a lumpen cautiousness, perhaps even a hint of the smug.

His days had a routine that had, unnoticed, become tolerable. His visits to the antique shop were easier. Small-talk revolved around sales, finds, bargains. There were endless turns that could be done: lifts to book sales, furniture to be carried, counters to be minded while he, or they, stepped out for a moment. The detail of the ordinary had small but persistent consolation. Becky's visits were regular. There were always vegetables to be admired and accepted, news of the boys' achievements and adventures to be recounted. The children had become accustomed to him and he had listened to their chatter about their father without flinching: the doings of a distant relative. His nightmares were not fed by any contact with Simon, who managed to be out on the rare occasions that Geoff visited. He passed hours at a time without thinking of drink, and only when he was near a pub did the familiar nagging ache return. The swimmer had faded, the image of her no more than a transfer on glass, like the snowflakes that shopkeepers of the town had stuck to their windows. Custom had increased to the point where he was always busy. Tasks of tidying, checking stock, paperwork, filled the evenings. Jenny and Olivia prevented a decline into dogged repetition.

He replaced the books on the shelves and took down his overcoat and scarf. At the other end of the town was a shop that sold local crafts. He had passed it often and noticed the window display, well-lit in a façade painted navy blue with gold stars. The woman behind the counter wore long earrings and a crocheted shawl. The handwritten sign on the wall above her suggested possibilities: Ulrike's wreaths, Didier's candles and honey in pots by Marie-Noëlle; Monica's batik scarves and ties and more.

'We have so little left,' the woman said, pleased. 'Is it for your wife?'

'Friends. Two friends.'

'I still have some jewellery.'

Malachite and lapis lazuli beads nested in velvet hummocks beside mother-of-pearl and glass earrings in a display case like a fish tank. Through half-closed eyes the colours might have been scales of mackerel. Geoff shook his head and concentrated. Olivia always wore pale colours. He pointed at a narrow silver pendant with a moonstone. Jenny wore deep reds and rusty browns. When the woman was drawing up the moonstone, he saw in the corner a brooch labelled 'cornelian'.

'That too,' he said, 'please.'

While she laid them on sheets of tissue and folded them into decorative envelopes, he looked around. Something for Seán? He hesitated. Hardly necessary. But Jenny and Olivia had been so kind and Seán was Olivia's son. A mug? He looked at the gritty sand-coloured mugs then picked one up. The handle was uncomfortable. He put it down and seeing the woman's stretched smile of tiredness, picked up a packet of long, beeswax candles. She rolled them in several layers of tissue and the fringe of her shawl dipped into the till as she felt for change.

'And for yourself, happy Christmas,' she said, tucking a sprig of holly into his lapel.

Carol-singers were warming up their voices on the bridge near the fish shop. Someone had hung wreaths on the tubular steel bars of the bridge and left a note on yellow notepaper: 'Large £5, Small £3.50. I am in the coffee shop, defrosting.' The wreaths were funereally dark. The shop where he had bought Tom and Stevie's presents was depleted but a few children were still peering into doll's houses and fingering sealed packets of electronic toys. The neon lighting was shadowless on violent yellows, greens and purples of synthetic goods. Flashing lights and hectic rhythms pulsated out of the video shop. An old woman waited by the door for her grandchildren and watched the flickering discoloration of the window display where *A Christmas Carol* was framed in tinsel with soft-porn and action movies on a bed of simulated snow. The pavement near the supermarket was clogged with people standing in twos and threes, talking. The airport minibus unloaded yet another score of emigrants, exhausted, struggling with huge parcels, dragging nylon hold-alls from the luggage bay and falling into the arms of waiting friends and relations. Geoff edged around the groups, stepping off the pavement and nodding to the people who greeted him.

Unnoticed, he had become part of the town. The newsagent and the greengrocer and the bank teller addressed him by name within days of his arrival. The custom of being saluted by every passer-by no longer surprised him. The only direct questions had come from Jenny. His association with Becky and Simon had been enough to establish him to the satisfaction of the town and he had never been required (and had never wanted) to say more. His only social effort had been to join the Kino Club where, once a fortnight, twenty or thirty gathered to watch 16mm films. On his first visit he had arrived late and had sat at the back. When the reels were changed he had looked around and assessed the faces, voices and accents. Most were from other parts of the world. They were polite but distant, chatting in ones and twos. The common wish to see films was sufficient, no other explanations were needed. The renting of a house had been the official seal on his presence.

The window of the antique shop displayed a crib: painted wooden figures in a small forest of holly and ivy. Nightlights in tall glass globes gave a soft harmony to the group. The bell brought Jenny to the door.

'Just in time,' she said. 'It's been a long day and now, at last, we can relax.' She took his coat and scarf and lifted the curtain for him to go through but as he moved towards the stairs she stopped him, lowering her voice. 'We have an extra guest. Seán's friend. I'd no sooner collected him from the airport than he set off to meet her at the ferry. That island, y'know, Inis Breac.' She resumed her normal tone. 'But you must meet her.' She opened the kitchen door and a flood of light, spicy smells and music met them. She nudged him into the room.

'Say hello. Our next-door neighbour, Geoff. And this is Bridget, Seán's friend.'

'Birgit.'

She was standing behind the table with a knife in one hand and the other resting beside an enormous flatfish. She laid down the knife.

'You are from the bookstore? Yes? We have met.'

Her hand was cold and, though she had wiped it on her apron, damp. He coughed.

'I – um, yes.'

He could see now that her eyes were green. Her hair was tied back in a plait that came over one shoulder.

'And she's cooking for us. Turbot, isn't it?'

He looked at the monstrous fish with its warty grey skin, a camouflaged creature exposed. He could think of nothing to say.

Seán was at the door and Geoff and Jenny worked their way past.

'We'll look forward to it,' Jenny said. 'And Seán, you know Seán? He's doing the rest.' She swept up an open bottle from the table and they went upstairs.

Olivia was hanging silver icicles from a tree. She stood on a chair reaching for a high branch. Jenny sat into an armchair, sighing pleasurably.

'She knows she's not supposed to. Heights and so on. But she won't fall, will she? You'll catch her, won't you?'

Having laid his parcels under the tree with the other presents, Geoff stood near the chair and looked up.

'I could do that if you like, if you've had enough?'

She looked down. 'I'm almost finished but there's plenty of other things. Or you could just sit.'

'And have a –?' Jenny waggled her glass. 'No? Not even at Christmas? Well, you're an example to us all.'

He could catch the dry, beckoning smell of red wine from where he stood. He looked into a white box where glass balls were packed in tissue. He unwrapped one. How simply it would shatter in his hand. He could just pinch it between finger and thumb and its cold reflected life would implode. The tree, the room and his miniature self, a distorted bespectacled manikin, would disappear. He hung it up and unwrapped another.

Jenny had finished her glass and poured another. Her cheeks had grown pink. She gazed benignly at Olivia.

'That pair. They *are* a pair, are they?' She tilted her head towards the kitchen.

Olivia paused, her back turned and an icicle dangling from her fingers. 'Are you asking me?'

'Well he seems very keen.'

'I don't know. There have been so many. Girls like him. They're intrigued by him and his life. He can seem somehow ephemeral. For one who is so practical, in reality.'

'Disappearing act: now-you-see-him-now-you-don't. But he *is* smitten, isn't he?'

Geoff waited, slowly folding the pieces of tissue and dropping them into the box. He could not decide if they had forgotten that he was there.

Olivia continued, 'I used to think that sometimes with some of the others but now I wonder if it's just my imagination. Wishful thinking. She's a kind girl and so pretty, why wouldn't he settle down?' She hooked the icicle onto the tip of a branch. 'Let's not say any more, let's just hope.'

She stepped down and began to move the chair to the other side of the tree.

'There she goes,' said Jenny.

'I can reach,' Geoff said. 'At least let me do that.'

Olivia nodded and put aside the chair and picked up another box. They worked their way around the tree, Olivia directing and Geoff easing the fragile ornaments onto the branches. As he touched the tree's needles, their resin slipped into the room. The faint sound of a carol service came from the kitchen. Olivia switched on the tree lights and stood looking at them.

'Well! Beautiful!' said Jenny, looking around. 'Just like the old days. Except for the children. That's all that's missing.' She chuckled. 'And I suppose, to be honest, it's much more peaceful without them, wouldn't you say?'

Geoff picked up the litter of twigs that lay under the tree and put them on the fire, then stood watching them flare and hiss. There was silence and then Jenny said, 'But of course you're seeing your grandchildren tomorrow, so you've nothing to be maudlin about.'

'Geoff might like some fruit punch –' Olivia was folding tissue paper and closing the empty boxes. 'Wasn't there some?'

'No I –' Geoff tried to refuse but Jenny was on her feet, putting down her glass.

'Made it myself. How could I have forgotten and this the season of remembrance?' She left the room.

Geoff stared at the flames. Shapes could become pictures, people, even, for those who believed. The flames remained flames. Olivia smoothed a sheet of wrapping paper. 'Jenny's always so cheerful, even when she doesn't feel it.' She paused, looking at the pattern of foliage and ribbon. 'It has become habit. Sometimes I'm afraid it's for my sake. It's hard on her, you know, playing the Merry Widow can be quite a strain.'

'It's hard on both of you,' said Geoff, watching her, slight and pale, even in the tender light from the tree.

'Well,' she looked up slowly to where he stood leaning against the mantelshelf. 'Harder on her. She has to live with an invalid. No, don't say I'm not. The thing is, I don't think of myself as one, even when I'm ill. But she must wake up every day in dread.'

'No! How can you be sure?'

'I know her well. Believe me, *I'm* the optimist. I open my eyes expecting sun every morning, while she –'

Ivy trailed from a bowl on the mantelshelf, moving in the heat from the fire. He stayed the fronds with his fingers. 'She is whistling in the dark?'

The door opened and Jenny came in, followed by Seán with a tray and Birgit with a parcel.

'The slaves are having a breather,' said Jenny, as Seán put the tray on the low table before the fire and poured punch from a cut-glass bowl with a silver ladle. Jenny and Geoff sat on either side of the fire. Seán and Olivia shared the sofa after Birgit had seated herself on a cushion on the floor, leaning against the sofa, next to Seán. She reached over and put the parcel on Jenny's lap. 'From my grandmother. This is the right time to open it, I think.' The parcel rattled.

'But is it for me?' Jenny paused in unwrapping.

'For the whole house. Household? Wherever Christmas is celebrated.'

Seán handed Geoff a glass of punch. It was dark red and had fruit floating in it. At least it was harmless. Geoff took a sip. Sickly sweet. He longed for a cigarette.

Birgit and Seán clinked their glasses. The last of the wrapping paper fell away and Jenny opened a box and, with some exclamations, took out a small propeller and slim brass bars, four angels blowing trumpets and a candle holder. Tissue-wrapped candles were finally lifted from the box.

'A mystery machine,' said Jenny. 'How do you assemble it?'

Birgit put down her glass and set up the candle holder, slotting the four white candles into their niches. Then she balanced the propeller on top of the central shaft and finally settled the angels on top. One of the angels had a dull patch on its robe. Birgit looked closely at it, then breathed on it and rubbed it with her skirt. She looked into the shiny wing. It reflected back her gleaming face. She resettled the angel in its place.

'Well what a wonderful thing,' Jenny exclaimed. 'We raise our glasses to your grandmother.' They lifted their glasses, looking at the angels revolving above the candles. The aroma of the punch caught in Geoff's throat and he waited a few seconds then put down the glass and stood up. 'Must see to the cat,' he said.

'Don't be long,' called Jenny after him.

'Dinner ready soon,' said Seán.

Geoff stood at the door. 'Back in a moment.'

In his own kitchen he drank a glass of water to clear the punch from his throat. He had hardly pulled the door of the antique shop behind him before he was groping for his cigarettes. He stood at his back door inhaling and waiting for the cat. He tried not to think about Christmas Day. He called to the cat and finished the cigarette, looking into the dark. There was no response. Perhaps if he left the door open. How brown that fellow was. Seán. It made his eyes, whatever colour they were, seem brighter and his hair unseasonably light. Of course she'd like him. Love him. And had she? Damn it to Christ Almighty, why did *these* pictures come so easily to mind? It would be no time before he would hate the pair of them. Were they a pair? None of that gentlemanly stuff about her sitting on the sofa while Seán insisted on

84

making do with the floor. No, he'd just slung down a cushion from behind his back and she'd hitched herself onto it without comment, the folds of her blue dress falling over his shoe. At ease together, that's what they were. No need for words, movements would do. Her shoulder almost touching his knee.

He went through to the front of the house and let himself out into the street, slamming the door behind him. He lit another cigarette and strode away from the town centre. In an archway two shapes were lying, malodorous bundles of rags. Two men, perhaps. One had a bottle in a paper bag and was attempting to drink. The other tugged at the bottle and some of the alcohol spilled. One good reason for drinking alone: no waste. He walked on. When he finished his cigarette, he turned. On the way back he saw they were still there. They wouldn't feel the concrete beneath them by now, nor the cold exhalations of the river. They'd forget everything except the bottle in their hands, the flattened wrinkles of the paper, the solid assurance of the hard glass underneath. He could join them. Get a bottle and then he'd be welcome. No. No sharing it. He walked on. A bottle on your own. An eternity of consolation. Transfigured into blackness. No better solution. No other solution, for as long as it lasted. Well, it felt like eternity, that was the thing. It eliminated the rest. Snuffed it.

When he reached his shop, he saw Dundee's face looming through the glass. He opened the door and the cat fled away towards the kitchen. He put food in the dish and poured milk. Had there been a faint smell of perfume from Seán, or was it his imagination? He had not noticed any on Birgit. If this were the kind of house that always had a bottle at the back of the cupboard. One mouthful would see him through the evening. The cat had had a few sips of milk and was dedicating itself to the food. No pretence there. No lies, no self-deception. With luck he would not be sitting next to Birgit. No time for another cigarette. He pulled the blind down just far enough to decapitate his reflection.

The kitchen table was round. Seán sat opposite Geoff with Birgit on one side and Olivia on the other. Jenny was between Geoff and Birgit but he could see her and when Jenny leaped up to fetch something, as she frequently did, he glanced sideways at her hands. Her wrists were narrow and her nails had rims of orange paint.

She stood up in a sudden awkward movement, when the turbot, on a flowered platter, was set down in the centre of the table and Jenny handed her a fish slice. As she lifted back the skin it resisted and he heard her draw her breath sharply. She muttered something and then the skin peeled back in a heavy moist flap. He wanted to look away. The thing seemed so murdered. But he watched her hands gently separating portions of flesh and blinked as the fish slice trembled. Could she be nervous? He looked up. Pinpricks of sweat gleamed on her forehead. She rubbed at them and her hair with the back of her hand and gave him a faint, embarrassed smile. The wad of fish fell from the slice and was fielded by Jenny with a plate. 'The one that didn't get away!'

Olivia and Seán laughed and Birgit relaxed. 'As if cooking it wasn't enough, we make the poor girl perform,' Jenny continued.

'I've never served it before,' admitted Birgit.

'The skill is in the cooking,' said Seán.

Birgit blushed. 'Turbot cooks himself. The art is to serve him.'

Jenny patted her arm. 'You sit down, love. I'll handle the beast.' She took the fish slice and aimed it like a sword. Geoff watched as a plateful of roughly hewn flesh was planted before him. Vegetables were spooned onto the yellow puddle of sauce and he picked up his fork. How wonderful it would have been to discover that he was not the only one at the table who needed a shot of spirits to calm quaking hands.

The fish was a success. 'Marvellous', 'wonderful', 'delicious', the adjectives sparkled over the bones. It came to his turn. His mouth was full. He nodded violently. 'It's –' he mumbled thickly, then clearing his mouth of food, 'exquisite.'

Exquisite. Where had that come from? Hardly apt for a dead sea monster.

He glanced at Birgit. Jenny's arm, planting a bottle on the table, came down between them. The plundered remnants of the fish were removed. Cheese and fruit were put in their place. Food provided another satisfactory distraction. Jenny stood beside Geoff and poured coffee into a small cup. She put her hand on his shoulder. 'We'll take pity on you now.' Startled, he glanced up at her. 'You've been deprived long enough. Seán! Where's the Duty Free?' A carton of cigarettes was put before him. 'And you can light up now. Yes! It's Christmas.' Geoff's hand automatically went to his pocket. His thanks were waved away. 'Seán always brings things.'

'Is it time?' Birgit looked around the table.

Seán bent towards her. 'I have something special for you.'

She laughed. 'I'm afraid mine is not at all special.'

'Should we bring them down?' Olivia asked Jenny.

'No, let's go up. It's more comfortable around the fire.'

'And this?' Birgit motioned towards the devastated table, 'we should –'

'Nonsense. The fairies'll do it.' Jenny led the way.

Seán brought the presents from under the tree. Geoff could not remember which of the envelopes was which. Olivia opened the cornelian brooch.

'Not for you, I think,' said Birgit quietly. She was sitting next to Olivia on the sofa. 'Not your colour.' They looked at Geoff.

'She's right. You're right. That's Jenny's.'

While Olivia opened the other envelope, Jenny fastened on the brooch, smiling and patting it. Seán was trying on a jumper, his head erupting through the neck. Jenny threw a lumpy parcel across at Geoff. 'Yours is the winter version,' she said. He opened the parcel and looked at the dark green garment, holding his cigarette away from it. 'Later,' said Jenny. 'You can try it on later.'

'You are much too good,' said Geoff. Birgit smiled at him. 'It will suit you.'

'I'm afraid I have nothing for you, I didn't know –'

'Not to mind. I have something for you. Seán told me.'

Seán handed her a flat parcel which she opened. 'Not wrapped, I'm sorry. I put them all together. This one is for you.'

It was a sketch of a thorn bush, the branches in black ink bent over to one side, the sky a violet wash. The pencil caption read, 'The Sway of Winter'.

The others were exclaiming over their drawings. Geoff shivered. The cold of that sky. He glanced at the window where the curtains were drawn in artless sunny cheer. He looked down at the picture. No one should be out on such a night. 'I'll frame it,' he said. Seán leaned over. 'Mm. A thorn bush. Mine's a plough. And what did you get?' He turned to look over Olivia's shoulder. Geoff looked at his drawing and closed his eyes. The violet sky became yellow, like the curtains. The wine-fed voices were full of contentment, pierced by little exclamations of pleasure. He stood up.

'Excuse me. I think I left the back door open,' he muttered. He closed the door and went downstairs and out through the shop.

What had come back to him was not an image but a sensation: that of lying on hard ground with the cold coming through numerous ragged coats. The newspaper lining getting damp. The irresistible chill. He hastened up the street to the archway. He bent down and, finding an arm, tugged it towards him and put money into the hand.

'What? What?' The form struggled to take shape. A bearded face thrust up from the rags. 'Whassat?'

'For Christmas,' said Geoff.

'Would'je get us a bottle?' The note was pushed back to him.

He stood up. Of course. No pub or off-licence would let them past the door. Too dirty. Too embarrassing.

'Would'je?'

He took the note. Already it stank.

McCormick's bar was packed. He had to hand the note over the heads of people to a young barman with white eyelashes and point to the top shelf where the brandy was kept. The noise was overpowering. He pushed his way to the door where more people were forcing their way in. The streets were emptying, people hurrying home. The shops were almost all shut and only around the doors of the pubs were groups gathered.

A squad car came slowly past him, then paused and reversed. A young guard leaned his head out of the window.

'D'je see the oul fellas?'

Geoff bent towards the bright eye, cocked between the upturned collar and peaked cap. 'Sorry?'

'Cuppla boozers on the tear.'

Geoff straightened up and pretended to consider, then said firmly, 'No. Never a sign.'

The eye gleamed. 'Great. We can knock off so. Have a good one.' The window rolled up and the car sped away.

When he reached the archway, it was empty. He looked through it and followed the small path down to the river. The grass on either side was clipped short: there was nowhere to shelter. He went back to the street and looked up and down. He turned around and considered the yawning, malodorous space. A crumpled six-pack carton and some caved-in tins were all that remained. He took the bottle from his pocket and placed it near the wall. Then he returned to the antique shop.

The door was on the latch and though the bell sounded, noone came to intercept him as he climbed the stairs. At the sitting-room he paused then opened the door gently. Jenny was asleep, her glass beside her, half full. Olivia was listening to music, her eyes closed, one hand touching the moonstone pendant. Seán and Birgit were on the sofa, talking. Her hair was loose and she had an amber necklace of large oval beads around her neck. She was holding up a loop to look at the fire through them. Seán spoke: 'Another tribe believes that you have to wear them when you are dead – twenty-nine of them, one for each of the spirits that you will meet in the afterworld.'

Geoff closed the door and went downstairs. In the kitchen he started to collect plates and glasses from the table. He filled the sink and rolled up his sleeves. When the draining board was full, he looked around and noticed a dishwasher. Sod it. He took a cloth from the bars that swivelled out above the sink and dried his hands. His coat and scarf were hanging on the hall stand. He released the catch on the door and heard it lock behind him.

He lay in bed and concentrated on sleep.

Had anyone ever listed the side-effects of sobriety? Merciless alertness, for instance.

Swearing, he got up. He threw a jumper around his shoulders, found his cigarettes and went to the sitting-room. The television was broadcasting Midnight Mass, faces ecstatic, over-awed or contemplative, children with candles: their faces, their faces. He changed channel. A hero was closing his mouth on that of a heroine. Quickly, he changed again. The gunfire of a Western was illuminated by Christmas lights strung across the street outside his window. Goodies and baddies, all in the same rosy glow. He heard a siren in the distance. The tedium of the screen was overwhelming. He started to doze.

He awoke in dread. The film was over, the screen dead. He was cold. He had the certainty that something had woken him. He looked out of the window. The street was empty. He went downstairs and checked the rooms. He found only the sleeping cat and the pile of presents that he had ready for the next day. He felt a coil of fear tighten inside him: a whole day with his son. The undisturbed order of the house brought neither comfort nor distraction. He looked at his watch: 3.15. He went again to bed. He could think about tomorrow or he could think about Birgit. Birgit and Seán. He had probably put the necklace over her head, separating it from the clinging hair, settling it around her neck so that the largest beads hung lowest. That must have been when her plait had come loose. He might have felt the softness of her skin. Tomorrow: Christmas Day. That would fracture any lust. He fell into a tense sleep and woke again, stiff and cold, in the same position. What side-effect of sobriety had caused him to leave the bottle? Lunacy? If so, temporary. He dragged himself out of bed.

The desertion of the street made him seem furtive. He heard his footsteps too loud, hurrying. Light from shop windows moved across him like slides on a carousel: The Fugitive of Christmas, A Picture of Evasion, something from Dickens. The bottle was gone. He turned and strode back. Five-Star High Dudgeon in the dawn of Christmas Day.

9

When Margaret arrived on her doorstep and pronounced the sea calm enough for a crossing to Oileán Cré, Birgit was too surprised to do more than agree. She rubbed the paint from her hands, put on an extra jumper and her coat and scarf, and put a pad and pencil in her pocket, while Margaret, having refused tea, waited outside. Her husband had the boat ready at the slip: a turquoise punt with an outboard engine that caught the first time he wound the cord around and whipped it off. No speech, nothing less than a shout, could be heard above the palpitations that reverberated off the rocks. The journey was only fifteen minutes.

Oileán Cré, from Birgit's door, was a line of uneven brown with a streak of cream for the sand at its rim, now separated into strands of grey, green, yellow and the tawny blots of dead bracken. As the boat neared the land, Margaret pointed to the flat top of the island where a handful of gables and chimneys began to define the skyline.

'I always know I'm home when I see those.'

'You lived here?'

'I was born here. I never left it until I was married.'

They landed at the little jetty that had been patched with concrete. New, sharp steps rose up to a well-kept path of flagstones which ended at a stone house. They walked past it.

'Millionaires,' Jerome said. 'Summer visitors.' Locked shutters covered all the windows. The doors were padlocked. 'There'd be a fear of thieves,' he said. Following him, Birgit could not tell if he was being ironic.

They skirted the beach and climbed the path that led away from the plateau where animals were brought out from the mainland to graze in the summer. The land fell away on either side of the road, a rough hilly path whose stony surface was softened by clumps of grass. They passed a few houses with creepers holding the stonework in place and roofs long fallen in. Their footsteps and breath sounded loud. Once or twice, small birds rustled through the gorse and fled behind boulders or deeper into the undergrowth. A slipway served by the mainland lay at the other end of the island, and around it, a handful of houses, more substantial than the rest. 'Newtown,' Margaret called it. Jerome led the way towards her father's house up a boreen wide enough for two to walk abreast. Birgit and Margaret trod in the old cart tracks and waited while he unlocked the yellow door.

The room had an air of transition, clean, furnished with a table, some chairs, a bench and a dresser but no curtains or cushions and a bare concrete floor. A staircase with graceful spindles rose into the corner opposite the door and was lit by a small window on the return. The walls were papered in cream aged to brown and patterned with a faded net of flowers. The only ornaments were a calendar and a scalloped oil-cloth along the edge of the mantelshelf. Margaret saw Birgit look towards the calendar.

'Twenty-six years since she died and he came to live with us.' She took a duster from her pocket and wiped the table and chairs. Jerome was at the hearth rolling a newspaper into spills. Then he took an armful of small branches from a pile and struck a match. The flames quickly reached up and he laid half a dozen briquettes from a stack against the wall, propping them carefully in the flames. He got slowly to his feet and rubbed his hands on his jacket.

'The nephew sometimes comes here in the summer with his family. They like the place as it is. We open the windows in spring, light a few fires in winter. Then he paints the windows and doors in the summer. The young ones draw water from the well.' He looked at the fire, unsmiling. ''Tis all a bit of a game to them.'

Margaret went upstairs and Birgit followed. The banister rail was shaped into a smooth curve that ended in a post with a round knob on the top. Each of the three bedrooms contained an iron bed and a mattress. The largest had a wardrobe whose door stood open. Margaret rested on the edge of the bed, her feet stretched out on the floor, one arm propped on the frame. Birgit stood by the window and stooped to look out.

'At night you could see nothing, the dark was that great, when there was no moon. We used to wait for Christmas Eve and then all the candles would be lighting. That was the custom. I could never get used to it on Inis Breac. Jerome used to wonder why I'd look out of the window when all we could see was the ocean, but here we could see the candles on the mainland and we would watch all night. It was like a miracle, so much light.'

Jerome coughed downstairs and Margaret pulled herself to her feet. Birgit squinted through the window at the overgrown hedge and the bay and beyond that, to the houses of the mainland, no bigger than the specks of salt on the pane.

'And you?' she said.

'Oh yes, we had them too. We'd draw up sand from the beach and my father would put candles in jam jars and pack the sand in tight around them. We were only young.'

The heat of the fire rose up the stairs as they came down. Jerome was on a chair with a sheet of paper spread at the table.

94

He glanced at them and continued reading.

Birgit went out and walked around the house. At the gable, a horseshoe was cemented in between the stones. A tuft of old rope straggled from it. The ruins of an orange cart lay against the gable. Three outhouses with descending roofs bounded the small yard, connected to the house by overgrown stepping-stones. At a gap in the perimeter wall she saw a shape, linear against the rounded forms that composed the landscape. She pulled back the grasses and tried to hold off the living and dead briars with her arms. It was the remains of an old plough, half buried. With care, she eased back the tangle that clothed it until the whole frame was exposed. She gazed at it, then, taking the pad and pencil from her pocket, made a few quick sketches. She heard the scraping of a chair in the house and the door opening. She finished her drawing and put the pad back into her pocket.

Margaret was putting a guard in front of the fire and Jerome had bundled the newspaper away onto a pile in the corner. After they had pulled the door to, they stood and looked at the roof, checking the slate. A transparent column of smoke still rose from the chimney when they turned back down the lane.

They could see the turquoise punt, a bright splash that came and went with the rise and fall of the road. They climbed down the meadow onto the rocks to cross the beach that lay beside the jetty and came close to another ruin that earlier, Birgit had hardly noticed. Only the empty remnant of a bell tower showed that it had once been a church. Hardly bigger than a house, its roof and the wall nearest the sea were gone. The churchyard ended at the point of the highest tide. The cross-section of green above and brown below edged back farther every year. In the sandy soil, Birgit saw random white marks, chalky hieroglyphs in the crust of pebbles. Margaret turned away.

'The sea will take all those graves in the end.'

She led Birgit up to the innermost part of the churchyard over fallen tombs dappled with lichen and broken kerbs buried in grass and wild flowers, to where a small stone, one of a few, stood erect over a neatly kept oblong.

'My grandparents,' she said. She placed her hand on the gravestone then looked across to the town on the mainland. 'Mam and Dad died in the hospital. They're buried beside the cathedral, where we'll go, I suppose.' She looked down at the grave. ''Twill be a long time after that, that the sea will take these.' She pulled a few strands of coarse grass away from the stone. Jerome, puffing, reached them.

'This land all belongs to that man over there.' He lifted his arm in the direction of the shuttered house. 'We wanted to ask him if we could build up the wall but he's selling up, the agent says.'

Margaret said nothing. Jerome turned and made awkwardly across the lumpy strip of ground.

''Tisn't right,' he muttered.

They followed him in silence to the boat.

On Inis Breac Margaret and Birgit set off for home while Jerome made the boat fast and talked to the ferryman who was cleaning his engine.

Birgit helped Margaret set the table, putting out plates of ham, lettuce, tomatoes, beetroot and hard-boiled egg. Birgit cut the soda bread while Margaret made the tea, swilling hot water in the metal pot and throwing it out the door before dropping in four spoons of tea-leaves and filling it up. She poured milk from a plastic carton into a white jug with a blue band. Then they sat down by the fire and waited for Jerome.

'My grandparents were the last to be buried on Oileán Cré.

96

Inis Breac never had a church and all belonging here are buried on the mainland.'

'What will happen to your house?'

'Another niece will have it for a holiday house or maybe she'll sell it. I don't rightly know.'

'I'm sorry. I shouldn't have asked you.' Birgit saw her neighbour's inward-turned expression. But Margaret suddenly chuckled.

'Sure, when we're gone, what'll it matter to us?'

The clock on the wall ticked softly. Jerome's footsteps sounded on the path.

'At Christmas,' Birgit said, 'do you light candles all over the house?'

'We put one in the window, for old time's sake. Sure, with electricity now, isn't it Christmas all year round?'

Soon after they had finished eating, Birgit walked back to her own house. Jerome's black-and-tan collie crept beside her to the end of the lane, then sat watching as she walked away in the moonlight.

Dear Seán,

This is one of the sketches I made a week or two ago and it's not good but it is a reminder of a day at Oileán Cré with the neighbours. All is changing so much here. Older people are very quiet, taking care of things that matter to them, and there are no young people. Margaret and Jerome travel every Sunday to the mainland to go to 10 o'clock Mass. The library opens for them. They meet friends and relations but they are all back here by lunchtime. I asked if Colm, the ferryman, could run a later service but Margaret just stared at me and said that he had to have a day off too. This made me think of our conversation when you wondered if I was lonely. No – I am not, still not but perhaps it is because of Margaret and Jerome, especially Margaret. I might never have become close to her if the island was full of people or if we were on the mainland. Perhaps most of my 'friendship energy' goes towards her. The island puts a ring around everything, makes it more intense. The simplest action becomes significant and nothing can be taken for granted. So I am lucky and grateful for the good fortune of her friendship. This is a small page from my pocket sketch-book, so there is no more room.

I hope you will have a happy Christmas with plenty of sun, or is Christmas celebrated where you are? Anyway, Bonne Noëlle, Frohe Weinacht, Nollaig Faoi Mhaise. Birgit.

Simon had hung white bulbs on a fir tree in the garden and the boys had insisted on lighting them, though in the bright sunlight of Christmas Day they were outshone. He had spent much of Christmas Eve working on a treehouse for the boys, while Becky distracted them with tasks indoors.

Geoff could see them from the window, climbing, waving their arms, handing up tools and pieces of timber, Simon occasionally swinging one of the boys down from a branch and the bulk of the hut a solid shadow in the constant movement of branches and figures. He had offered to clear the table but Becky wanted to rest and in the clutter of the kitchen he could not move without disturbing her. Spiced beef and a demolished goose lay among the remains of the vegetable dishes. The paraphernalia of the meal had spread to cover every available surface. On the table itself were the scalloped peelings of the tangerines that the children preferred to Christmas pudding. Tom had practised juggling with them, getting four into the air before the golden loop had shattered and the fruit had tumbled about on the floor, to be chased by Rex and Stevie.

Geoff turned from the window and bent to pick up a tangerine that had rolled into a corner.

'Geoff?' Becky's voice came from the sitting-room. She was

stretched in one of the armchairs beside a small fireplace where a dense red fire made the room very warm. 'You're not?' she appeared in the doorway.

'Tidying? Oh no, just looking and thinking.' He held out the orange. 'They used to be wrapped in silver, each orange like a treasure, and we only got them at Christmas.' It was such a small comfort and yet it nestled potently in his hand. She leaned against the doorframe sleepily. 'Mm?' She smiled. 'And now they come in plastic nets.' She took his arm. 'Do I have to force you to sit down? Or,' she glanced over her shoulder towards the window., 'would you prefer to be out with the boys?'

'No, no. They're happy as they are.'

He went with her into the sitting-room and sat on the other side of the fire, reaching up to put the orange on the mantelpiece. Cards crowded it and more hung on ribbons on either side, moving with every current of air. The snowy landscapes, laden trees, candles, cribs and stars held no recollection, none that he knew to be his own. The orange sat at the end of the row like a full stop. If he pushed it nearer, might it not strike a spark from those sentimental scenes? A paper-chain reaction? A snowball of memory?

'You look happy,' Becky murmured.

'Do I?'

'And now you sound surprised.'

'Yes?' He looked around the room, at the ivy trailing along the picture rail, the tall candle in the window, the scatter of toys and books on the floor, to the relaxed affectionate gaze of his daughter-in-law.

'Take it where you find it,' she said.

'Mm?'

'Happiness.'

At lunch he had taken refuge in quietness, passing plates,

food, trying to merge unseen. The boys' liveliness had helped and his interest in them provided a simple tactic to disguise his evasion of Simon, who might almost have been colluding with him, energetically moving, organizing, helping. That was it: movement. Simon, when Geoff was there, never stayed long in any one place. His manner towards Geoff was polite, almost vague. The children, preoccupied with each other and the excitement of the day, did not see, or did not find disturbing, the constraint in their father's manner. Neither a barrier nor a bridge, they were an innocent buffer, carelessly at home with both generations.

'Geoff.'

'Mm?'

'You're thinking too much again. Here –' she picked up a stray cracker and reached across the fire to him. He took the frilled, slightly battered end and they pulled. There was a crack, the contents flew into the air. Becky fielded something, a green bullet. She prised off the elastic band and put the tissue-paper crown on her head, then handed a small red cellophane fish to Geoff.

'You hold it in your hand and it tells you what you are like.'

He held it in his hand and she read from the paper slip. 'If the head curls up you are passionate. If the tail curls up you are cold. If head and tail curl up, you are jealous. Which is it?' She leaned towards him and they watched as the fish twisted. 'Hm. Nothing here about that, but wait.' She turned the paper over.

'What am I?'

'You are ...' She became solemn. 'It says you are Made in Japan.'

They laughed. He wanted to prolong the moment but the footsteps and the cries of the children sounded on the path leading to the front door.

The boys tumbled into the room, their cheeks scarlet, their clothes full of chill, loamy smells.

'Dad says ...' Stevie gasped for breath, 'he'll clear up and then we'll go for a walk.'

At the word, the dog flexed into the air as if electrocuted and tore out of the house, barking. The boys flopped onto the floor, tearing off scarves and hats, and wrestled with one another. Geoff held the fish, watching the boys, while Becky picked up the twisted fragments of the cracker, threw them on the fire and got up. The foil and crêpe caught with a soft sound and then made a banner of blue and gold. Simon was in the kitchen. Slowly, Geoff rose and picked up a couple of mugs and a plate and brought them from the sitting-room, stepping carefully around the boys.

The lake was almost a mile from the house, with wooded hills to the west and high farmland to the east. The road from the north was narrow, curving and hilly. The boys, on their bicycles, rattled ahead of their parents and Geoff, pausing with one foot on the ground to look back at each corner. When the road rose, Tom strove to cycle to the top but Stevie struggled until Simon caught the saddle and helped him. Becky and Geoff carried the kites that Geoff had bought as Christmas presents and the dog wound ceaselessly through them like a live copper wire. The descending sun brought the hills into relief, emphasizing every small contour, setting the haws on top of the hedgerows ablaze and intensifying all the colours, the greens and browns of the fields and turning the pallid grass into white gold.

'Fionnán, it's called,' Becky said. 'Fair.'

Clare: Clare lying in a field sleeping, on a day so still that he had to hold his breath to hear the grass move, one arm shading her face. He had wanted to touch her hair and lifted his hand then stopped, not wanting to disturb her.

'Geoff,' said Becky, turning to look at him where he had stopped. 'Whatever is the matter?'

He lowered his hand and dropped his gaze. She came and took his arm, looking up at him. He cleared his throat and shook his head.

'It was nothing,' he mumbled.

'But –'

Her arm grazed his and the kite strings threatened to become entangled. He started to separate them, concentrating on the task. Ahead of them, there were shouts of laughter. It looked as though Simon was trying to race Tom, urged on by Stevie, with Rex bucketing about dementedly then running under Simon's feet. With a shout Simon fell and lay laughing on the ground while Stevie dropped his bike, ran and threw himself on top of him shouting, 'Tom's won! Tom's won!' Tom wheeled around and cycled back, with Rex making feints at the glittering spokes of his bicycle. Becky and Geoff caught up with them and Becky dusted Simon's jacket and hair, joining in the laughter.

They moved on up the next incline and then, at the top, caught their first glimpse of the lake, a shaded triangle, in the dip between two hills. The boys coasted down and rounded the bend with Simon calling after them to be careful. There was no traffic moving but when they rounded the corner at the foot of the hills, they saw a small handful of cars parked in a lay-by, directly opposite the low stone wall that bounded the lake. The road bordered the lake on two sides and then disappeared into the trees. A man with a white terrier on a lead was locking his car and, dimly visible among the trees, a family was walking towards the farthest point where the road veered away steeply uphill. Stevie and Tom had dropped their bicycles and were leaning over the wall looking down into the shallow water, counting sea urchins. Stevie's toes were barely touching the road and Becky held his shoulders, sitting beside him. The lake appeared to be enclosed by land, but a hummocky island at the far end hid a narrow inlet through which the sea forced itself in a powerful surge that weakened when it reached the broadness of the lake, making the tidal movements slower than normal, giving the shallows the stillness and clarity of a prism. They watched the purple spiny creatures, waiting for, imagining, movement. Long, combed strands of seaweed hung down from the walls. The children finished their count and started to search for crabs. From above, the water was only visible when it moved, but far out from the shore the sun caught it and turned it into a blinding platinum. Towards the deep centre of the lake, the surface reflected the blue of the sky. The sudden hills threw dark shadows all along the western shore but the east was in full sun and the fields were solid, massed colour, speckled with sheep and cows and a few glimpses of houses: a chimney here, a gable there, or just a spire of smoke like pale grey wool. They walked as far as a white gate, where the road ended. They glanced up at the empty house, surrounded by rhododendrons, then turned to look out over the lake to where the sky gave clues to the invisible sea beyond it: seagulls, a sprinkle of brilliant specks, far up, almost invisible, birds of the imagination. Stevie watched them, murmuring to himself, while Tom flicked pebbles into the water. Soon, the sun would disappear behind the western hills whose abrupt rise made them seem darkly monumental. Stevie shivered.

'Right,' said Simon, 'let's climb Knockdara and fly the kites.'

Rex materialized and shook a hearty spray of water on them. The boys grabbed their kites and swooped back along the road, almost colliding with the man and the terrier. Rex and the terrier made tentative acquaintance and moved reluctantly on.

The boys leaned their bicycles against the ivy bank where the hill path started. The almost vertical rise had been made accessible by the laying of a forestry trail whose compact surface was easy underfoot. It rose in a zigzag of short stretches with occasional steps of wood, and seats placed where walkers could regain their breath while looking down on the lake. The darkness of the woods became a mottled, multidimensional pattern of bare cramped oaks, shining holly and magically upright rowan and pine, the trunks lost in a bed of brushwood, ivy and fallen leaves. Becky and Geoff brought up the rear, with Stevie clambering breathlessly ahead of them and Tom following Simon, who had already disappeared above. Soon the three were well ahead. Their voices floated down like leaves, frail and sharp in the chill, still air. Rex plundered the undergrowth, tantalized by countless spoors.

Geoff and Becky sat on one of the benches. The hill, when they glanced up, never seemed to get smaller, being so steep that only the next few yards were visible, and the short twists of the path, with its sudden turns, made them almost dizzy. They looked down on the lake, which had shrunk to a remote, bright snapshot.

'I could just stay here, gazing,' Becky said. 'This must be what the birds see.'

Out on the water, a rowing boat was an indigo spot. Something, a shoal of fish or perhaps the boat itself, had made a path through the water, a polished arc that belied movement. Above them was silence. Geoff lit a cigarette and they watched the smoke's plume dwindle to nothing.

There was a rush and a crackling and suddenly one of the kites, purple and yellow, swooped down before them, hovered quivering, and then soared away up and out over the lake. The thin screams of the children were joined by a shout of triumph from Simon. Becky and Geoff stood and watched the triangle of colour and its long streamers probing the sky like a jellyfish idling in deep water. They hastened up the hill through the hanging branches that obscured the last few yards of the path. Then they were on open ground, heather-covered between jutting shoulders of rock, on the exposed summit. Simon had handed the cords to Stevie and was hurling the second kite into the air. It caught an up draught from the hill and was almost torn from his hands. The red and green box shuddered once and then flew companionably on the same current as the first.

'Let me! Let me!' Tom shouted.

Simon handed him the controls and stood back. To the others, holding their breath, it seemed as if the cries of glee came from the dancing kites whose invisible cords anchored the children to the hilltop. The sun was almost at the horizon but here the light had gathered and concentrated, leaving the lake in complete shadow, a nether world of winter.

Simon glanced around. 'Where's Rex?'

Geoff and Becky unwound kite streamers from Tom and looked vaguely at him. 'We thought he was with you.'

Simon shook his head. 'Haven't seen him since – when was it, boys?'

They did not hear him. Stevie ran to Geoff and hurled himself at him, clasping him around the waist.

'That was the best Christmas present ever!' he shouted.

'Yeah!' Tom grinned.

Still holding a kite, Simon stood and looked at Geoff, surrounded by Becky and the children, closely gathered behind the red and green kite. The last rays of sun caught them then the horizon rolled it up, like a blind.

'Right,' said Simon, 'someone's got to find the sodding dog.' He whistled, then, laying the kite down, started calling Rex, turning like a town crier to send his voice over the lake and hills, then he started down the path. The others followed.

They reached sea level in minutes, the ground tumbling down before them, seeming to drag them with it, getting faster and faster until they stopped, breathless, beside the bicycles. Simon had gone on towards the lake but as they started after him he turned and waved them away. 'Go back! Go back!' he called and then stopped as Becky ran forward, awkwardly clutching a kite.

'Simon, let's all look,' she said, 'that way we'll find him quicker.'

He shook his head. 'The boys will get too cold,' he said. 'If I'm on my own Rex will come to me. He won't think it's another game.'

She stood and watched as he strode away. The boys stood watching until she turned and then they guided their bicycles towards home.

The kitchen with its gleaming plates and red curtains, the sitting-room with its latticed fire-screen and stirring ivy, even the stairs and the deserted upper rooms – all wrapped tight a welcoming drowsy heat that they breached with a draught of sea-dampened coats, voices carried in visible plumes before them and a careless relief at the ready comforts of home. Becky shuffled a tin of mince pies onto a plate and put it in the oven. She filled the kettle and drew the curtains. The boys lay on the rug before the fire and set out a board game, rattling dice and sending miniature explorers into crocodile swamps and snake-filled jungles, while Geoff folded back the screen and revived the fire which had settled into one clogged ember. He swept the hearth and picked up twisted scraps of paper, the sundered strips of bangers and discarded crowns. Then he lit the candle in the window and pinned up a frond of ivy that had fallen over the doorway.

It was amazing how easy it all was, a revelation, that peace was not a single entity but a whole collection of small movements and sounds and specific, noted moments which would cling together and, in recollection, form one solid ember. He stretched his legs out before the fire, lit a cigarette and listened to Becky pouring water into the teapot and the boys scuffing the mat with their feet, clicking the dice and urging on their chosen pieces with elation or dismay. He looked at the two heads bowed over the board and then went into the kitchen to carry the tray of steaming pies and tea.

When the boys tired of their game, Geoff took down the Junior Memory box and he and Becky watched, incredulous, as the boys scattered the cards face down, and then Stevie, after a few turns, easily matched the two-dozen pairs of flowers, shells, vegetables and fruit. Tom laughed but had to have another try, so the cards were shuffled and spread out by Becky and he stared at the uniform backs, willing them to guide his hand. Without apparent concentration, Stevie won again. Becky tousled Tom's hair. 'It's old age. You used to do it more easily.'

'Once I start thinking, I get confused,' said Tom.

They played Animal Families and Becky and Geoff allowed themselves to be beaten. The candles shone with translucent brilliance on the gleaming backdrop of the darkened windowpanes. A breath of wind played in the chimney and Stevie looked towards the fire and then at the unwavering candle-flame.

'Where's Dad?' said Tom.

'He'll be back soon,' said Becky and sent him to switch on the outside light.

'I thought the candle was supposed to light the traveller,' said Stevie.

'Well, two lights will be twice as good,' said Becky and suggested another game.

The boys could not agree and Becky sent them to put on their pyjamas, promising that Geoff would read to them. They rattled off upstairs and she turned to Geoff.

'You don't mind? It's just that they're tired and they won't sleep until Simon comes back.

'Mind?' said Geoff, 'I won't mind,' matching her casual tone with care. 'But,' ordering concern into his voice, he pushed himself up on the sofa where he had been slumped, 'is it late? Should we worry?'

'No. Rex's often been gone longer. It's just that he spotted a would-be pal, the little white terrier, remember? And there are sheep on the hills. Simon worries but you mustn't.' She pressed him lightly on the shoulder. 'You stay as you are. I'll get hot chocolate for all of us. If he's not back in half an hour, I'll drive down for him.' She went into the kitchen. The boys scuffed about upstairs: light padded footsteps, giggles, a tap running, the flop of a towel on the bathroom floor, mild cries of protest. Geoff stared at the fire and listened, quelling his breath, straining to hear any sound from outside. The soft noises of domesticity pattered on, trickling into the arid crannies of his mind. He wanted to slide right down into the battered sofa and let the entrancing drift of sounds settle on him like feathers from the beaten cushions. He closed his eyes. The sounds continued. And then he could not bear it any longer. He had to get up and cross to the window to stare out. His reflection, uplit to a mobile caricature by the trembling candle-flame, stared back at him, tense, frowning, fearful. He squinted past it, trying to see in the livid outside light that draped itself across the garden wall and onto the grass, a dull half-hearted wash, like the failure of all colour. Neither movement nor sound came to him from outside and the glass clouded as he muttered, 'Just half an hour. Just give us half an hour more.'

He started back as the boys rushed downstairs with great thumps from short legs on steep risers. Becky followed with the chocolate. Tom chose a large, new book and they settled in with

Geoff, crowding up to his sides, each holding the book with one hand and a mug with the other. Geoff put an arm around each of them and started to read. After two pages, Stevie, his eyes fixed open, was drooping onto his chest. The fire, Becky's intent face leaning on her hands, the rampage of silly animals on the boys' pyjamas and his own voice, formed a tight enclosure that excluded everything else. It was not until the latch on the outer door was lifted that the spell broke and then the boys were gone from the sofa, the book fell from Geoff's knee onto the floor, Becky stood and Rex rushed in, followed by Simon.

'Careful! He'll knock the mug,' said Becky, smiling up as she bent to save it.

The boys clambered over the dog, pummelling him, chiding him.

'And now it really is bedtime,' Becky said, gathering the boys. Tom started to protest but Stevie fell into her arms.

They went upstairs and Simon put the soaked dog in the back porch to dry. Geoff remained in the sofa, unable to move. He felt a chill on his sides where the boys had rested. Pages of the book slipped over with a muted flutter and he hauled it back onto his knee without thinking. Simon was in the room again.

'What a picture you made,' he said from the doorway.

'Mm?' Geoff angled his head, pretending not to have noticed. 'Sorry?'

Simon, in his socks, moved to stand in front of the fire, his back to Geoff.

'The three of you, all cosy on the sofa there.'

Simon looked over his shoulder, stretching his numb hands to the fire.

'Quite the little family.'

'Simon –'

'Yes, that's me, got my name right.'

'Simon!' Becky's voice was sharp from the top of the stairs. 'Come and say goodnight!'

He left the room.

What were the words for escape? Geoff looked around for clues and saw only a small room, untidy with happy accumulations of the day. The sheer bland normality of it all: it gave nothing. The interloper would have to find his own language.

The door of the boys' room shut and he heard Becky say in a tense whisper, 'Don't spoil it, don't!'

'Go back to the boys,' said Simon.

The footsteps came downstairs and then he was in front of Geoff again.

'You recognize me now, do you, after all this ... this ... *time*.'

Geoff was sunk forward. Simon reached down and gripped his hair and pulled Geoff's head back. They stared at one another, an exchange of rage and fear, and then Simon let go and, rubbing his hand on his jumper, started to pace awkwardly the cramped spaces of the room.

'What d'you think you're at? What d'you think you're doing? What?' With each question he turned and glared at Geoff. 'You want my house? You want my wife?'

'Simon!'

'You want my children? Is that what you want?'

'Simon, the boys –' Geoff tried to indicate their nearness, in dread that they would hear.

Simon's voice became a ragged hiss. 'They're mine. Don't you dare try to shelter behind them. You've wormed your way in, you pathetic old fraud. You had no time for me.' He gave a bark of laughter. 'Christ, I used to wonder what was wrong with you. Weaving and wavering about with shaking hands. Dropping your cigarettes. I thought I was well shot of you when you took yourself off finally. And just to be sure, to be sure to be sure, I brought them all here. *My* family. After Sadie died, there was nothing to keep us there. Nothing!' He was in front of Geoff, spitting the words down on him.

Geoff fell back on the sofa, looking up at his son. That face, those eyes, the way the brows were shaped, just barely angled up and then down, like wings.

'Clare,' Geoff whispered. 'Clare! You look just like her.' He gave a faint laugh. Simon was rigid. Geoff leaned towards him. 'It's that you never, you never ... look at me.'

Simon looked dazed.

'And now that you do, now that you are looking at me, you look like her.'

Simon snorted in contemptuous disbelief, and turned his head away.

'Her face: that same beautiful colour, when she was agitated. And she always looked at me directly, like you, like you were, just now.'

Simon turned his head slowly back to stare at the floor just in front of Geoff's feet and Geoff saw all the colour drain from his face. The image of Clare, the molten obverse of her radiance, died.

'You. Are not wanted. Here.'

Simon walked to the door, stepping on everything in his path. The book, the lid of a box of games, made small crushed protests. The tail of a kite slipped briefly across one heel and Geoff saw that he had a hole in his sock. He pulled the door vaguely after him and padded slowly upstairs. The bathroom door opened and closed. So soft. All so soft.

Geoff waited for a moment and then struggled to his feet, levering himself up with his hands. He picked up the lid of the box and fingered the split corner, then let it fall and took up the book and touched the spine where it had been torn. He put the book on the mantelpiece with some others, easing them into a symmetrical pile. He looked around the room, scratching his head and sighing, then went towards the open door and stood for a moment at the foot of the stairs. Becky's voice was a murmur in the otherwise silent house. A movement near the back door caught his eye: the dog had raised his head and was looking at him.

With great care he opened the door, stepped out and closed it noiselessly behind him.

II

December 27th

Dear Oma,
So you had Christmas at home. I am sorry I was not there, it sounded so cheerful on the phone. No, I could not come but how would I be missed when there was such a crowd in your apartment? I can just imagine you around the table with candles and angels. The ones you sent me were perfect and I was glad to light them in the company of friends so that I was not too lonely when I thought of all our Christmases. No walks in snow-covered parks here! The town is grey, though there are lights, but the music over loudspeakers plays to empty streets: a stage set for something that does not happen and the sea does not know there is anything to celebrate.

I had two whole Christmases. Seán collected me on Christmas Eve and I cooked fish for him and his mother and aunt, Olivia and Jenny. It was good but I was so nervous. I had a sudden feeling, sitting at the table, trying to divide the fish as you do it, that

I was being displayed to the family. At first it didn't seem to matter. We were comfortable by the fire. His mother is a lovely woman, sometimes ill (he doesn't talk about it), but not now. But when we were at the table I thought, perhaps this is not friends sharing food, but me performing for Seán's family. Seán did not say anything beforehand, the invitation was sudden, almost a command. Jenny came to Inis Breac, to my door.

'He can only manage two days' leave,' she said, her eyes moving around my small paint-spattered room as though there were nothing she could look at and still be polite. But a week later, when Seán met me at the ferry, everything was fine. He was so brown, coming from a place where there is no need for fairy lights and complex festivities. Or so I imagine. It must have been that man, their friend, Geoff (did I mention him?), the bookseller. He was there too. I have met him before but he is distant. He seems to have difficulty finding words and the ones he finds are not quite right, as though another conversation was happening in his head and he cannot stop it. A sort of aural equivalent of double vision. He is not unfriendly but his presence is not complete. I make him sound mad, someone who hears voices, but he is not mad. How can I explain? Do you remember the paintings of Paula Rego? Sometimes the sitters look at ease. This is intentional, I'm sure, but sometimes those stiff poses and anxious eyes suggest that they have had too much time to contemplate their appearance: they know that their discomfort is being immortalized.

Is that it? Is he so much at odds with something, with himself, with life, that he is never quite present, never there in his own skin? So different from Seán. And yet, given something to do, he is almost at ease. He lit the candles on your angels with just one match. When he wrapped the books for me he put them in several bags, very neatly, to keep them dry. For someone tall, he moves lightly, though he is more often still, not like Seán.

I cannot tell you how much at ease I am in Seán's company. It is as though we were born friends. We can disagree with ease too but without dislike. They each had a sweater as a present from Jenny and Olivia. Seán's was of linen: very light. He swam into it like a fish. Geoff looked at his in deep green wool, its arms folded in cruciform, and almost seemed not to know what it was. Perhaps he is not at home with things, despite the candles and the wrapping. Or maybe it is the kindness he cannot enjoy. A gift: friendship made concrete. Or perhaps he just didn't like it? They did not try to persuade him to put it on. They understand him, I suppose. And he brought them lovely jewellery, so exactly right for each (they are very different). He doesn't ever seem to look at anyone directly, or for long, so how does he learn about other people? Through his nerves? Like antennae? Seán is so uncomplicated, it is a relief. But Geoff almost choked when he tried to speak. Poor man, made speechless by private misery. He went away quite early, I can't remember when. I was too fascinated by Seán's stories of the people he lives with. He looks like someone from another planet. We are all so pale and huddled in our wintry lives.

Next Day

Nonsense! I was tired and yes, cold. The stove had gone out and I was sitting so close to it I think it was *me* keeping *it* warm. And if you could see the sky now: a blue so brilliant it looks as though it has just been invented. I won't re-read what I've written, one glance showed the name of Seán too often. You will worry. You will fear that I am about to dive into his life without a thought. But no. History won't repeat itself. And I did NOT dive into Peter's life, I sank slowly. It closed over me without my noticing. And for proof: Seán is gone. He had two days, but only one with me, the 24th, and then I spent the 25th with Margaret and Jerome as I had promised.

She spread the table in her kitchen with a cloth that her aunt sent, thirty-four years ago. (Her aunt was a missionary nun. There is a photograph of her on the mantelpiece in 'The Room'. She is wearing a white robe, just turning yellow, now, but always perfect, like the past, whether good or bad.) 'The Room' is where we were to eat. She said, 'We'll dine in The Room.' It is a parlour with a rocking chair, anti-antimacassars, prints of saints and children, all in a veil of romanticism, a carpet, a cactus that looks as if it is part of the plot, the artifice: never to be watered, never to need water or air. The fireplace with its immaculate conspiracy of fake coals, ever red, had just been switched on when I arrived. The warmth was imperceptible but it was burning that fine coat of dust that, even with Margaret's attention, had succeeded in landing. I begged her not to lay the table in 'The Room', I said I would not feel like a friend but merely a visitor. She understood straight away and relaxed. What would have been an ordeal for both of us became a pleasure. But the embroidered cloth was draped upon the kitchen table just the same and the butter was put in a silver dish with a lid and the sugar in a great cut-glass bowl like a chalice, right there, so exactly in the centre of the table. We had turkey and ham and sprouts (you know, like dwarf cabbages), and potatoes boiled and roasted. Even Jerome seemed content. Shep was allowed to lie on the floor in the warmth. Even the cat was tolerated.

Then Jerome went for a walk and Margaret and I washed the dishes. She put everything into the white porcelain sink and poured boiling water from a gallon saucepan on top, with some crystals of soda. Then she beat the plates to cleanliness. No, she scrubbed them and yet with such energy, she is so small, her arms are like sticks, her hands are shining pink, the pads of her fingertips are cracked, her shoulders without flesh, like a wire hanger on which something too heavy has been hung. The washing-up was like a battle: so much noise. Margaret won, of course.

And then we sat down by the fire – a small furnace in a heavy enamelled metal box, in industrial fawn, with ovens and hot-plates: an omnivorous monster that sits in (has eaten?) a huge hole in one wall, without grace or ornament, but so warm. We stretched out exhausted beside it like two Pliocene explorers beside a sleeping dinosaur and heard the clock tick and the dog sigh and she told me that this was the best Christmas she'd had in years. They could go to her niece on the mainland but Jerome won't, so they are always alone.

I was ashamed of my present: a small painting, but she patted my hand and told me that I was the best gift they could have, and then I felt even more ashamed. I had not bothered to change my clothes. The same blue wool skirt that I wore on Christmas Day, my hair unwashed, my hands paint-blotched still. I looked down: I could see a sprinkle of oil on my shirt. I was a scruffy, second-hand offering but Margaret smiled. Her eyes shone. All that work, plucking and stuffing and sewing and scrubbing and peeling and basting, was worth it, it seems. I had nothing to say. Does living on your own make you selfish? It hasn't made *you* selfish.

The night, as I walked home, was black and silver. There was clear, clear sky over a sea that looked like frosted glass with silhouettes of two trawlers on a triangle of ocean. It is nonsense to say the light was dark but it had no colour. The shapes became flat. Everything was in two dimensions, except that I was there too. Trying to flatten it and contain it (as when painting, or when talking about it, like now) is a bit like making ice-cubes: the compression of something wonderful, alive, into little trays.

As the fire, the welcome as warm as the fire, the

house, the dinner, the glowing windows and the soft footsteps of Shep faded, fell away into the dark, the dark itself became a huge presence, swallowing the land and sea and sky and laying triangles of silver, strips of black, oblongs of dark grey, that filled my head all night. I had drowsed in Margaret's kitchen. By the time I was in my own, I was totally awake. And so I started to write to you. And then I could not sleep.

She laid out two tubes: black and white. She dipped a large brush in water and blotted it on a towel. She squeezed a worm of black and a worm of white onto the enamel plate. Then she scooped the white paint onto the brush and spread it on the plate's centre and diluted it with water. Next, she washed the brush, dried it on the rag and took a speck of black and mixed it, swirling it deep into the white, until a very faint, even, grey pool, thin as cream, lay on the plate. She took up a white board and very quickly coated it with the mixed paint. She balanced the board on a grill rack over the stove's hot plate. In a few minutes, warm and slightly bowed, the board was dry. With a pencil, she made a quick outline, trying to recall the shapes of the hills, the broad scroll of the water bounded by the horizon and the irregular geometry of the trawlers. Something was missing, but now, in daylight, she could not check. She eased the board flat and started to paint. She filled in the sea's triangle with dark grey, then the sky with paler grey, then the foreground of the hills with black. Then she went over the sea, using her smallest brush, to put in countless black dots. She repeated this with white. Then she concentrated more white near the horizon. She stippled in the hills with black, layer on layer. Very carefully, she painted in the trawlers with smooth strokes, building up a solid shape for each.

She put the board up on the table, propped against a chair, and stood back to look at it. The sense of purpose trickled away. The painting, in its simplicity, had exactly failed. Nothing of night, nothing of the suspension of day and its colours, none of the dramatic force of so much exclusion, was shown.

She opened the back door and threw out the painting. It fell among dead nettles, face down. It was dusk.

She opened the stove's door and threw in kindling, sticks and lumps of driftwood. The smoky roar of the fire was a pleasant diversion. She slammed the door and threw on her coat. Then, as night grew up around her and the hills, the hedges, the roads, the sea, she walked all over the island.

The night might have been an exact copy of the previous one: a belated gift. 'Look,' it seemed to say, 'it is all still here.' But each of her senses was now alert. She could see the black, the grey, the silver, but it was no longer a pure and perfect vision. Now she heard the sea, felt the dip and sway of the grassy tracks, smelled the shore's tang, almost tasted it. In the thickening layers of night, she felt as small as a moth, as vulnerable as a caterpillar. What had been missing from her painting was everything. To copy nature was a waste. Nature already existed, perfect in its own imperfectible way. One had to ... to what? To select? Had she not already selected? No one could accuse her of placidly committing shapes to a flat surface and hoping that they were in some sense true. Exhausted, she found her way home and fell asleep in a chair in front of the hot stove that, to her eyes, seemed to pulsate.

January 2nd

Dear Oma,

I am sorry about the silence. You do not reproach me, but to have two letters from you when I know how much your hand hurts, is a reproach. I am so unsettled. I cannot concentrate. I tried to paint the sea by night and failed so badly. The last time I saw the painting, I turned it over by accident with my foot, one night, when I was stumbling about in the garden, looking for something (inspiration? the ash bucket?), and next day it was face up to the sky. The weather had curdled the pigments, or corrupted them. The humiliating thing to tell you is that it was an improvement. The mess is now sinking into the soggy ground, like a crooked tombstone in an old graveyard. For days I have not been able to paint. I still cannot. But at least the weather is now changed and I am spared those perfect nights that were the beginning of my failure. There may still be some hope (that I give up or that I start again, you will not be so unkind as to ask).

Margaret has been so kind. I called in on her on one of my walks (for days I have been walking), and she said that not being able to paint is the most natural thing in the world. 'The hens do not lay at this time of year. They have no mind for it when the sun is that low,' she said. So I had to laugh. Have I brought on my own collapse by trying to paint while the sun is low?

Yesterday, when I called, the door was open as always but Margaret was out and the bucket was gone from beside the door. She must have gone to the well (she always uses fresh well water for tea), and at first I thought I should follow her but then I thought she might meet someone there and want to say something private to them, so I waited. She was gone a long time and I walked around the kitchen, not wanting to sit before invited. The door to 'The Room', was open and eventually I went in.

There is something about an unused room. I don't know what it is but it was not present on Christmas Day. We had banished it with our talk, I suppose. Yesterday 'The Room' was full of its own spirit. With stiff-backed chairs, one on either side of the fireplace, and china cabinet and ornaments on the mantelpiece, it might be a stage-set but it holds none of that promise that the empty stage has before the action begins. Here is no action nor possibility that anything may ever happen. Margaret may add another ornament or replace the coloured grass in the big oriental vase that stands in the corner, or even, yes! water the cactus, but not in expectation of events to come. The chairs will not sag and sigh, relieved of their burden, the leather pouffe will never betray the presence of tired feet. 'The Room', never animated, will never fall silent.

But it is not a museum, not even one of those rooms in Folk Museums, where objects come from different sources but never achieve a unity because they are unrelated. The rocking chair, rescued or taken from its real home, never belongs anywhere else. And yet we look at it and are moved and sad because we know it once had a place, a place of its own, a life and a meaning in lives not ours, but, in ways, like ours. From the rocking chair with its expectantly plumped cushions, we miss the occupant, which (our sentimental hearts would tell us) was old and beloved. What is wrong in Margaret's 'Room' ('wrong' is the wrong word: *different*), and here I am guessing, what is different is that these chairs, this little table have never been used. The pictures have never been anywhere else, never moved to a better spot, seen only as part of 'The Room'.

There is something strange in the preservation of things new: a knowledge that not using them will not prevent them from getting old.

As I stared at the furniture, the rocking chair with its intensely polished, unblemished rungs, where feet should have worn a bow or dip, and the ends of the arm-rests, which hands should have burnished to a softer shine, I suddenly thought of someone terminally ill, in intensive care, minded, pored over, but required to do nothing, just to continue to exist. Perhaps 'The Room' contains Margaret's illusions, the arrangements of a life. As if she had, by dusting and starching and polishing and washing, managed to perfect one small piece of reality. And when I looked at how well she had succeeded, 'The Room' seemed enormous, a vast hall full of unique and priceless treasures.

I didn't hear her come in. It wasn't until she said, 'What's the matter, child?' that I turned and saw her in her navy-blue wrapover pinafore, all blurred, that I realized I had eyes full of tears. And so then

I blinked and started, and the tears fell and I could not persuade her that I was not broken-hearted over something else. (Poor Peter. He never moved me to tears.)

After handkerchiefs and mugs of tea, I was able to tell her that it was because 'The Room' was wonderful. She laughed and shook her head but she was pleased. And then we went for a walk in the cold and windy late afternoon and the astonished Shep (Margaret does not often go for walks, she has too much walking to do as it is) came with us and tried to catch the stones that I skimmed over the waves and then shook himself all over us and we came to my house to dry ourselves and him. Then suddenly, she was gone: Jerome's tea to be made; the hens to be shut in their house.

I had lit the stove when we came in and after Margaret and Shep left, I put my feet up on the chair where she had sat and let twilight become night. The stove was so hot and so closed up, I had neither the need nor the energy to do anything. Last night I slept well for the first time since before Christmas.

Love, Birgit.

I haven't heard from Seán.

Dear Oma,

You are not going to die. You are not thinking of dying. You are not. You are not. And yet you send me all this money, 'to be used now'. You don't want me to wait until you are 'gone'. So unlike you to use a euphemism. The first thing I thought was that I should go to see you: that would be my logic: no thought, just go. But you know me too well. I read on further and you say you do not want to see me. You make sure that I won't come by going away yourself. 'For a holiday.' You must be very well. But you are not all enigma and command. You say that I talk so much about Seán and see so little of him, that there is a danger I will create a delusion, something false that is less or more than the reality. But I think you are wrong. I like Seán, he is helpful and can make me laugh and he is leading a life that I find fascinating. Everything he describes, the place, the people, the work, what I tell you, I see through his eyes. I should like to see for myself, to know for myself.

So now what? I shall throw some summer clothes in a bag, shake down the contents of the stove and pull the door behind me, not lock it. There is no need.

That all sounds pleasantly simple. I suppose I shall have to root about and find some cotton clothes, then rinse and dry them. Then talk to Margaret and ask the postmaster to keep my letters. All those things that sound more like a good housekeeper than a traveller. But it will be such an adventure: it will! It will!

Fondest love, Marco Polo.

Margaret shook her head.

'You won't come back to us,' she said. 'You were happy here for a bit and then you grew lonesome.' They stood in Margaret's house. The old woman twisted a dishcloth in her hands. The dog watched, tense and still from the doorway.

'I will come back. Of course I will,' said Birgit, stroking Margaret's shoulders.

'I don't know will we be here,' Margaret said.

'But where would you go? Of course you'll be here.'

Margaret reassured her. 'Nowhere at all. Don't you worry. We'll not go anywhere. But you will come back?'

'Yes. Yes, of course.'

They hugged one another. Jerome came forward and shook her hand, almost causing her to cry out with the fierce compression of his grip, and they watched her go from the gate, Shep sitting beside them, soundless, unsure.

12

'You got my note?' Jenny was polishing the glass of a picture in the antique shop.

'You're good to come so soon. I slipped it in your letter-box first thing this morning. We're off, you see. Flibbertigibbets that we are.' She made a girlish pirouette with the yellow cloth above her head. 'On our travels, tra-la!'

He held the folded note between his fingers and watched as she dabbed at another painting, the portrait of a young girl seated at a table, light from tall windows behind her falling on her round cheeks, on her arm and hand, loosely resting near three or four peaches, and on her pink, square-necked smock.

'We'll be able to pick our own soon, or apricots, even.' She turned to face him. 'Don't look so glum. Yes, I know it's only the 26th but, oh the weather and the dark days ahead and we promised ourselves one decent holiday when we sold up –' she wrapped the cloth around a candelabrum, catching two corners and tugging, left-right, left-right, to perfect the shine on the base. 'But who needs excuses? Olivia's so well, so well! And here she comes, as proof!'

Olivia came in carrying a tray of glasses. 'I heard the bell and hoped it was you. Has Jenny?' He nodded. She laid the tray on the sideboard. 'Just putting these back after our celebrations.' She took the thin-stemmed goblets one by one and arranged them on a circular tray. She looked at Jenny. 'Did you tell him that Seán had gone?'

'He's gone ahead of you?'

'Oh no! Gone. Gone back to work, first thing this morning.'

'You want me to mind things here?' He had his back to the light. Jenny came to peer at him.

'That's what we were hoping. You don't mind?'

He shook his head.

'How was Christmas Day?' asked Olivia.

'Good. Very good. I was with the family, you know, the boys.'

Olivia came and sat on a low stool and looked up at him.

Jenny rubbed a spot on the window. 'But tiring, I always think, small children can be,' she pounced on another spot, 'so tiring.'

She looked across at him. 'You know we'll be shut. Nothing to do here, really.'

He tried to smile at her. 'I'll take care of the place and all these things. Too valuable to leave. Now where would you be without me?' Empty jocosity.

She caught his proffered mood. 'You are the sunshine of our lives,' she sang, waltzing towards the curtain. 'And now I'm putting on the kettle.' Her face reappeared with Pierrot comicality around the tasselled fringe. 'Or would you prefer moonshine?'

They gathered at the round table in the kitchen. The smells of spice and wine lingered and he thought of Birgit, her sleek head above the waves. Olivia brought the mugs from the hooks above the counter. In the recess below stood a decanter. It had a shining head and graceful shoulders and it was almost full of port.

'We'll be gone for a couple of months.' Jenny pushed a jug of milk across the table.

'Anywhere in particular?' He poured a thin stream of milk and watched it layer below the surface of the tea.

'No. We'll just find places we like the look of, places we've missed before. Drive into a small town or village, see if there's a restaurant and a little pensione, even just a house with a couple of rooms to spare. And then stop. Look at the church, they all have churches. Sit by the fountain, explore the market, if we're lucky enough to be there on the right day.'

Olivia passed him a spoon. 'The elements are usually similar but the details vary,' she said. Jenny continued, 'Take photographs. Maybe buy this or that for the shop.' Geoff's tea dipped towards the centre and grew opaque as he stirred.

'That'll be nice.'

Jenny munched a biscuit. 'Free as air. Nobody but ourselves to please.'

'That'll be nice,' he said again. He took the spoon out of the mug, waited until the drops had run off and laid it on the table.

'But what about you?' Olivia said. 'Will you be all right?'

'Me? Oh, don't worry about me.' He turned and saw the anxiety on her face. 'I've plenty,' he paused, 'plenty to keep me busy.'

Jenny stood up. 'My camera. Now where did I put it? Upstairs? Tch! I almost forgot.' She left the room, quizzing herself.

'We may not be away as long as that.' Olivia was still watching him. 'In fact I wonder if it's such a good idea to go for so long.'

'Your health?'

'Not that. I haven't been so well for years.'

'Is it ...' He cast about for an idea. 'Seán?'

'Not at all. He'll be back where he really wants to be by now. Well, almost. On the way, anyway. And we can contact him at any time, if we really need to. No,' she hesitated.

'The shop then. Is that it? I've told you, I'll –'

'No, no.' She cleared her throat. 'It's you.'

'Me?'

'We are friends, aren't we?'

He nodded, waiting.

'Well, friends should help one another and I get the impression,' she spoke fast and then stopped and took a deep breath. 'I get the impression that everything is not as it should be. Not right at the moment, for you. You and your family.' Her voice was almost inaudible.

'It's fine.' He clenched the mug. 'It's fine. Everything. They, all of them. Just –' he scraped back his chair.

'I'm sorry,' she said, looking up at him.

He put his mug on the draining board then picked it up, turned on the tap and swilled water into the remains of the tea. When he faced her again his voice had softened.

'They have their own lives to lead.'

She disguised her sense of defeat with an understanding smile. Their friendship was strong enough to bear the weight of superficial confidences but not for the more profound misery that he was doing his best to conceal. With time, but there was no time: Jenny's footsteps sounded quick upon the stairs.

'Found it! Old and a bit on the mechanical side, but still working. There's even a film in it.' She held it out towards them in proof. 'I am careless.' She started to rewind it.

Geoff moved away from the sink.

'Going so soon?'

'I'll let you get on with your packing. Give me a shout when you are ready to bring down your bags, and don't forget the keys. I'll need a set, as Janitor-in-Chief.' He attempted to grin.

In his own shop he eliminated the signs of Christmas. He stood on the centre table and whipped the string of fairy lights off their hooks and dropped them on the floor. Then he ripped the rest from their clips around the window and door. He crumpled the publishers' fliers and cardboard pyramids and plucked all books referring to Christmas from the shelves and crammed them into boxes, putting the childrens' books at the bottom. The handmade cards from Stevie and Tom he slotted together and put in the back of a drawer. He took a bunch of holly and crushed it, crackling and pricking his hands, then forced it into the bin, ignoring the nail-scrawl of leaves on the lid, and swept up the trail of blackened leaves and blood-red berries that rolled and rattled away with a frivolity that he tried to quell with a brush.

The room had a depleted, wan air that settled on him more heavily each time he stopped. He looked at his watch: there was still time before he might be called upon to help. He opened the filing cabinet and made numerous changes, impulsive and superficial. At last there was a tap on the door and Olivia came in wearing a dark blue coat and gloves.

'All set?' he said and inclined his head past her, 'and the luggage?'

'Oh, Jenny has taken care of that.' She looked around. 'You've been busy.'

'Just getting things in order for, ah ... for the sale.' Even to himself this announcement sounded abrupt.

'Oh?'

'Yes. You know, after Christmas.'

'Oh. What a good idea.' She glanced doubtfully at the shelves, from which all signs of the past season or of future enterprise were absent.

'You'll make notices, I suppose. Posters, you know, on that sort of card with lurid colours, electric pink, or green?'

'Oh, posters, yes. Yes, of course.'

'Well, a notice in the window maybe.' The keys tinkled faintly in her hand and she held them up and then put them on the table. 'I wish,' she looked from the keys to the floor. 'I wish you'd let me help.'

'I –'

'Not with the sale. With whatever it is has gone wrong.'

The silence, tense, artificial, was fractured by the beep of a horn in the street. They both turned to see the car with Jenny leaning over from the driver's seat to look through the passenger window. Olivia moved away.

'We'll write.'

As she opened the door he moved to catch up and put his hand on her shoulder.

'Take care of yourself,' he said.

The passenger door creaked as Jenny opened it and pushed it out. 'We'll be back before you know we're gone,' she called. She tooted the horn twice and revved the engine and by the time the puffs of exhaust had vanished, the sound of the engine was distant.

They had put a small notice in their window: Back with the Swallows! He stopped and looked at it, held for a moment by its ambivalence, and then went in his own door and pulled down the blind.

In the off-licence the assistant, a tall, bony woman with shining coils of hair fenced by glinting steel combs, rolled four bottles of whiskey in sheets from the local paper and stood them in two plastic carrier-bags. Geoff re-crossed the street diagonally. A band of sunlight caught the west-facing roofs and deepened the shadow on the façades. Curtains were already closed behind the decorated trees and the single red bulb above the crib in the stationer's shone like an incubator. The cat watched distantly as food was put out in the yard: more interesting prey was caught between life and death in the overhang of the river.

There had been a message from Becky on the answering-machine since early morning. At times during the day, responses had revolved in his mind and now Geoff picked up the phone. Relieved to find himself speaking to another machine, he said in a clear voice: 'No need to worry. I just felt like a walk and yes, I'm fine. And thanks for everything. Yesterday was …' He paused. 'Perfect.' Another pause. 'Jenny and Olivia have asked me to go abroad for a few weeks, so I won't be in touch for a bit.' What more? 'And thanks again.'

He found an envelope and wrote: Closed for Winter Holidays, and taped it to the shop window, then pulled down the blind. The flurry of the morning had gone. From the moment that he could no longer hear the car he had moved easily in the blank space between possibility and its opposite. Vaguely he thought he could thank Simon for this weightless freedom that had a kinetic quality, like the shells and feathers which Stevie had hung on invisible lines that revolved, apparently at random, without any perceivable cause or aim.

Leaving the front of the house unlit, he closed the door between the shop and the kitchen and sat at the kitchen table.

At last, at last. The foil cap of the bottle sheered open with a snick of recognition and the whiskey uncoiled into the glass: the most reliable thing in the world. The flame that ran down his throat was a blessed torch that set fire to the past and the future and ended his uncontrolled speculation about both.

13

At first it was the smell, a mixture of cremated tarmac, fumes from the aeroplane and its attendant jeeps and buses, laced with a dry wind fanning over thousands of miles of nameless cities, plains and forests that hit the travellers when they stumbled out of their air-conditioned bubble.

In the terminal building there were no seats and the luggage took an unexplained forty minutes to appear on the carousel. Birgit wanted to lie down on it and circulate on its meandering course whose low buzz and vibrations would help her sleep. When the travel-battered parade of bags went back for the third time, the weariness of the passengers turned to anger. A man in a navy-blue suit snapped his car-keys together in his fist and waylaid a member of the ground staff. The staff man raised his eyebrows and splayed his hands, to placate and disown. The man in the blue suit turned to his companion and said, 'The wrong luggage, it seems. The airline will contact us if and when.'

The last stage of her journey brought back a sense of common humanity as the ancient bus, a haphazard assembly of metal sheets, wooden battens and rusty bolts, plundered the dark with the frenzied uncertainty of an unbroken horse whose only interest, upon first feeling the weight of a rider, is to rid itself of its load. Luggage was fastened to the roof and every now and then a cry would go up, as someone saw a piece of their belongings slip its moorings and hurtle down past the window. The crush of bodies prevented people from falling out of their seats. Small boys sat in the aisle, holding smaller children on their laps. The woman beside Birgit had a huge cardboard box that cheeped and from its airholes, diminutive beaks poked. People smoked and someone passed around a bottle. When it came to her, she tried to drink but almost choked on the blistering spirit and, passing it back to the man behind her, knew thirst to be the core of her discomfort.

The lights in the bus failed and smells of warm flesh, livestock, and sweat competed with the sounds of laughter, snoring and the nasal rattle of a transistor radio. The heat was made bearable by the flow of air through the open windows, air thick with the scent of unknown vegetation, interspersed with the parched concrete of small towns. Towards dawn, the heat relented. The movement of the woman with the chicken box woke Birgit. She watched as the woman, hoisting a baby onto her back and a bundle onto her head, carried the chickens off the bus. Five small children followed, laden with parcels and bags. There were few passengers left.

Birgit moved up to the seat behind the driver and spoke the name of her destination over his shoulder. He glanced at her without reducing speed.

'Two stops,' he said, waving two fingers in the air. The bus attacked another pothole. He looked at her again, more slowly.

'Nurse?'

'Visitor.' She watched the road, willing him to turn back to it. 'Holiday. I have a friend.'

'Aha!' He roared with laughter. 'No swim. No ski. No five-star hotel.' He finally looked again at the road and continued to laugh. 'Hallooo, friend!' he crooned to the dust-crazed air.

A small group, barely visible in the pre-dawn light, stood waiting at their stop. As she stumbled down the steps, they started climbing aboard, then she was alone. Dust, mist and the fumes of the bus surrounded the village and filled its deserted centre. Beyond the huts, Birgit saw the branches of small trees and bushes. When the noise of the bus could no longer be heard and its exhaust was nothing more than a catch in the throat, she saw the outline of a well in the middle of the empty clearing. She thought of Margaret at the pump and the flood of crystal that shone out with a few smart thrusts of the handle. She leaned over the wall and looked down. No reflection met her eyes.

A cock crowed and muffled sounds of life floated from the huts. A door opened and then another. A woman stopped as the child she was carrying tugged at her and pointed. Soon there was a cluster of children inspecting Birgit. She looked down at her clothes: the sagging linen jacket, the sour white t-shirt, the universal defeat of her blue jeans. A travel-worn stranger was a novelty. One of them ran across the clearing and returned with a slender young woman who wound a length of fabric into a head-dress as she came. The children remained silent as the young woman said, 'You are Seán's friend?'

Birgit started to explain, pointing after the bus, as though it could be called back to verify her story then stopped. For a moment she had feared that they would have no common language and she almost laughed as she heard English. The young woman smiled, a slow warm smile whose brilliance lit up her face. 'He is not here. He had to go for water but you are welcome.' They shook hands. 'I am Nathalie. Come and meet my family. Seán will be back as soon as possible. Later today.'

She set off and over her shoulder said, 'We will have breakfast and then I must go – I teach – and my mother and sisters work in the fields, so you will have the house to yourself.'

Chengue, Nathalie's mother, was a stocky woman with a deep

line between her eyes. She poured a mug of water carefully from a lidded tin and handed it to Birgit. Neither she nor her younger daughters, Zizi and Amalia, teenagers ripe of flesh and sullen of expression, spoke, but a stool was provided and a bowl put into her hands. Once her thirst was eased Birgit found that she had no appetite, but not wanting to be impolite she picked up the spoon and ate the yellow mash, wondering what it was.

'Good,' she said.

Chengue's steady regard seemed to suggest that had she been able to speak English, she would have chosen a different word. 'Fodder' might have been more apt.

Nathalie went into the hut and came out with an armful of books. 'I've put out a bedroll for you. Rest until Seán comes. Please be comfortable.' She set off ringing a handbell that attracted a swarm of small children.

Birgit looked around the dark interior of the hut. Curved walls did not make the placing of furniture awkward: there was none. A neat heap of bedrolls and a transistor radio stood beside a black and scarlet laundry basket on top of which was a folded pile of t-shirts and fabric lengths that would become robes like the one that Nathalie was wearing. A saucepan, a ladle and a handful of cutlery lay on a sheet of newspaper. Hairbrushes, clips and combs and a few jars of cosmetics were arranged on an upturned crate in front of a mirror in a pink plastic frame. The walls were decorated with zigzags of reds, browns and deep yellows as free as her own dragon of painted paper sheets at Inis Breac but in bold, precise order. The thatched roof came down outside almost to the door, and the space between it and the frame was a mosaic of shards of crockery. At a glance she could see that the other houses, two dozen or so were similarly decorated. Similarly but not the same. Some continued the painted colours on the outside of the walls and put a border of mosaic all the way around, under the thatch overhang. Others confined the mosaic to a broad band around the door: each proclaimed itself part of the group but individual. She closed the door and lay down on the thin bedding, then, covered by darkness, she slept.

She had woken to a dim rhythm, familiar in its unmusicality. There was a sudden silence and then the saw-and-whinge restarted. The well, she thought. Who can get water from it? Adrift between sleep and wakefulness, she shivered.

She spent the afternoon sitting in the shade seeing the village activities through a hangover of sleep. Dozens of children perched on benches in a semicircle around Nathalie, under a tree whose leaves hung down lifelessly. On the other side of the clearing a row of men sat with their backs to the corrugated-iron wall of a shack, smoking and drinking bottles of beer. The open door showed others, shadows in the gloomy interior. An ad for Southern Comfort had been pasted to the door and another for Marlboro cigarettes had been stuck to the window. On the ground, in front of the hut that Seán shared with six brothers sat a frail-looking youth beside a heap of junk metal and wire from which he was making toy aeroplanes and bikes. His only tools were a pliers and a Coca-Cola bottle. Chickens picked in the dust at every house and one or two tethered goats nibbled at anything they could reach. A boy untied them and herded the scrawny animals away from the houses and into the bush. The queue for the well hardly moved. Beyond the village the land lay flat in all directions. Above the horizon was a line of low cloud that appeared and disappeared during the day, a threat or a promise of rain.

She was one of a crowd which turned out to meet the lorry. At the first distant sound, the women at the pump turned, the children scrambled into the branches of the school tree, Nathalie

139

stood too, men came to the door of the bar and one or two older people came to the doors of the huts. The noise of the engines grew and grew and then, preceded by billowing dust, a jeep and a lorry hurtled into the thronged centre of the village. The children dropped from the tree to claim the men who climbed down from the vehicles. A few men on bicycles came in from the fields, women running after them, hoes in their hands.

From the edge of the crowd she could see Seán jump down from the lorry and become absorbed in the moving press of people. She stood alone at the entrance of the hut and while the cargo of water was being unloaded she saw Nathalie take Seán by the arm and point towards her. He turned and stared, shading his eyes. She might have been a distant view, an unexpected vista dutifully indicated by a guide. He started towards her with the expression of a traveller seeing his first mirage, gazing as though, if he blinked, she might vanish. But when he reached her and threw his arms around her, she saw that it was Nathalie who had disappeared.

His face was grey with dried sweat and dust.

'I should have been here to meet you.'

'You have work to do – and anyway I was so jet-lagged all I needed was sleep.'

'Nathalie made you comfortable?'

'So welcome!'

Around them children made a moving circle, dipping forward, giggling, drawing back. A commotion started at the lorry and a small man came running towards them waving his arms. 'Charlie,' said Seán, then turning to Birgit, 'Two ticks.'

On a slight rise of ground the barrels were being lined up near a cluster of unfinished huts. Birgit had seen them, not so much unfinished as so little built that she had not understood their significance. Now, in what remained of daylight, men and women shovelled and turned the clay while young girls and boys poured the water. The long process of mixing the dry and the liquid to make a firm paste that could be fashioned into bricks occupied almost every able-bodied person in the village. Dust-coated and bent over in labour, Seán was indistinguishable from the rest. Birgit watched for a while and then began to shape bricks, working methodically, aware of her slowness.

Briefly, before night, the sun turned all the roofs to gold and the women went to their huts to prepare the evening meal. Birgit followed Chengue into the bush, picking up twigs and sticks, the brushy detritus of the landscape, useless for anything except kindling, so dry it was almost ready to light without the aid of a match. The length of dead wood with the charred end that had kept yesterday's fire going was shunted farther in on the circle of stones and soon the bark began to singe and peel. Chengue pushed a blackened pot into Birgit's hands and pointed towards the barrels of water. Birgit waited among the little group carrying their pots, and when it came to her turn, tilted the barrel but could not set it upright again quick enough and water splashed onto her foot, a pale accusing star on her skin. The others giggled complicitly.

After the evening meal, Nathalie brought Birgit into their hut and closed the door. Then she lit an oil lamp and placed a small basin of water, a cube of coarse soap and a rag on an upturned crate in front of her.

She cupped her hands in the tepid water and lifted it to her face. Then she trickled it through her hair and across the back of her neck. She took off her t-shirt and jeans and dropped them onto her jacket, which lay where she had left it that morning. All sensations of dislocation and unreality slipped away as the clinical wafts of carbolic drove out the sweat and the gritty residues of her journey. Nathalie sang a nonchalant song, rocking from side to side and the lamplight touched her shining forehead and the pearly curves of her shoulders. Her bangles made a faintly jangling, wayward accompaniment. Birgit picked up the cloth and dried herself. Hearing it rustle, Nathalie reached up and took from on top of the laundry basket a folded cloth which she handed to Birgit saying, 'This is your new gown.' Birgit wrapped the cross-hatched fabric twice around her and tucked the end into the upper border, to secure it. The indigo, white and black pattern dipped from her left breast to her right knee. As her body warmed the garment, the smell of vegetable dyes rose like night-breaths from the plants themselves.

Nathalie called in Zizi and Amalia and spoke to them, then she took a large jar and unscrewed the lid. Each of the sisters took a generous scoop and turned, beaming mischievously, towards Birgit.

'This is for the skin. It saves it from all weather and drives off the flies and all bugs,' declared Nathalie. She held out the jar and Birgit sniffed, a tangy resinous smell. Then they rubbed the paste into her hands, arms, shoulders, face, neck and feet, chatting and glancing at her. They massaged her arms with long strokes then combed her hair and twisted it back off her face. Free of its weight, her neck felt cool. For the first time she began to feel truly awake.

Before Seán arrived the girls dispersed. Chengue had been chatting to a neighbour and in her absence Amalia and Zizi had slipped out into the dark, and crossed the compound to the music and laughter of the bar. Nathalie picked up her bag and turned towards the door.

'Won't you come to town with us? We're going to telephone the airport about my suitcase. I am sure Seán –'

'No. Thank you, no. I have to teach – parents now. See you later.' She inclined her head and left.

The town was an hour's drive from the village. Birgit held on as the unsurfaced track buffeted the jeep. Seán looked across at her.

'Quite the local woman in those clothes – and here's me as scruffy as ever – didn't even change. You look beautiful.'

Birgit stood beside Seán in the phone booth at the Bar Lucille and listened to him speak, moving his free hand the way the village people did, like a conductor interpreting a score, urging an orchestra to a music that to her was still incomprehensible but now familiar. The shadow mimicked his movements, elongating and then foreshortening them. The voices on the phone changed, the crackle on the line remained the same, as though some giant insect had become impaled on one of the poles that stalked the landscape. He hung up and turned towards her, shaking his head. They went into the bar and sat at a low, flimsy table, preferring the uneasy squeak and quaver of wicker chairs to the sticky uprightness of tubular steel bar stools. A rotary fan in the ceiling tugged at sluggish strands of smoke sent up by the handful of drinkers. One or two turned to eye Birgit in the coloured robe that emphasized her foreignness. The slightest movement made their chairs creak. Seán leant forward, his forearms on his knees, his hands hanging loose.

'No luck, I'm afraid. It's one of those shift-work things. The people who were there when you arrived –'

'I understand.'

The mean lights of the bar made craters under his eyes and dry furrows in his cheeks. The lines of his forehead were like the fractures that scored the village fields.

'It is only a case. It doesn't matter. Thank you for trying.' She finished her drink.

'Another?'

While he was at the bar, she studied his back. The light shone on his head and shoulders, making him look stooped. When he turned around the tiredness of his face touched her. He set her drink before her and she waited until he was seated, then raised her glass.

'Sláinte!'

The unexpectedness of that familiar word made him look up. 'What'll we drink to?'

'To your success! To the completion of your lovely clinic.'

'Lovely?'

He reached across to touch her glass with his. They drank and then he laughed.

'Lovely! What a word to choose.'

'It is so much unlike any clinic I've ever seen (all antiseptic smells and cold surfaces). No child will ever be afraid to go into it. It will be more like a home, when it is finished.'

'Ah. When it is finished. When oh when.' He put his glass down.

'You doubt it?'

'We have so much trouble with water and the government is dragging its heels about helping. I should be used to this by now but it's a nuisance.' He rubbed his glass with his thumb and watched the condensation run down. She sought for some comfort to offer, something encouraging to say. The fan revolved at a tilt, with a repeated note like a faint groan.

Shouts and laughter in the street grew louder as a crowd of people crossed the pavement towards the bar. Birgit edged her chair closer to Seán's as a wedding party burst open the doors but though she raised her voice and he bent his head to hear, the celebrations swallowed her words. A huge woman leant her bosom on the counter and reached in to turn up the radio. A man with a white trumpet clambered onto the bar and began to play a ragged version of a popular song.

They finished their drinks.

In the street he held out his arm and she placed her hand in the crook of his elbow.

'What were you saying back there?'

The words that had come spontaneously to her now sounded lame but he said only, 'It is nice to have support.'

'Everybody in the village supports you.'

'Yes. Don't think I am not grateful for that but they depend on me. To some extent I'm seen as Mr Fixit. And that frightens me. They won't reproach me if I fail but their understanding is almost worse than a reproach. Failure never surprises them.'

'You won't fail!'

'If you knew how much I am tempted to walk away, sometimes.'

'You wouldn't.'

'No.'

They stopped at a window in a small shopping mall where a life-sized model turned blind eyes on a wide-screen television.

'Sometimes I only survive by not seeing what is all around me. It's relentless. The need. Needs. And the obstacles to doing even the simplest thing. I wish –' He tailed off.

'What do you wish?'

'I wish I was in Carrickfergus!' He hugged her. 'Do you know that song?'

He hummed a few bars.

'What is it about?'

'Longing to be somewhere else. Inis Breac. I wish I was in Inis Breac with you.'

They smiled at one another, hesitated for a moment and then kissed.

On the return journey the jeep bucked and swayed, a mobile drum, the empty rear amplifying the noise. When the trees thinned and bald patches of ground started to appear, he slowed the jeep and looked at her, his face ashy pale in the dark.

'We're nearly there. You to your female dormitory and me to my monastery.'

She turned towards him. His eyes were bright with tiredness, a habitual exhaustion overcome by will and force of habit. She put out her hand to touch his shoulder at the same moment that he leaned towards her. Their hands tangled as they kissed. The gear-stick, the reeking leather seat and the jutting dashboard snagged and hampered them. He took hold of her plait and gently drew her head away from his.

'In the back?'

On a ragged length of tarpaulin, they made love. Awkwardness and discomfort yielded to a sense that at that moment, this was what each of them needed. Above their heads, moths, seeking the quenched headlights, drifted and staggered through the open windows.

She awoke with a dim awareness that he was asleep. His unshaven face rested on her shoulder, his arms and legs a heavy yielding mass. She turned her head and immediately he said, 'Was I asleep?'

'We both were. For a little while.'

They moved apart, disturbing an insect that rose and flew, bumping a tattoo of panic on the roof.

'Some alarm clock,' Seán said, yawning.

The insect redoubled its attack on the metal.

'My God, is there ever a moment or a place where you can be alone?' His words were muffled as he dragged on his shirt. Then he pushed open the doors and Birgit fanned the creature into the night. It lumbered off and Seán slid out, reaching in to help Birgit. As she touched the ground she stumbled and then laughed.

'I thought it was someone come to check on us.'

'Our hosts? Charlie or Chengue?'

Birgit thought of Chengue. She would be lying in the dark, deeply asleep, sure that her daughters were packed tight, safe around her.

The village was still when they arrived. Seán brought the jeep to a stop a short way from the outer edge of the clearing. The paths were livid veins under the moonless, starry sky. He came with her to Chengue's door. It was a snug fit and once she was inside she could not hear his receding footsteps. Gradually she became aware of the soft breathing of the women. As she undressed she scanned the dark for any sense of disturbance, became aware of a tension and knew that someone was awake.

'Nathalie?' she whispered. There was no response.

'Can we talk tomorrow?' Again, nothing.

She was certain that Nathalie was lying, wide-eyed, staring into the blackness, subduing her breath, concentrating on being not there. She turned over and tried to think of Seán but could not focus on him, distracted by the intensity of Nathalie so close, so intent on withholding everything. She could not sleep. She felt around for her drawing pad. The pencil was jammed into the wire spiral. She sat up and balancing the pad on her knee she drew continuously, without lifting the pencil's tip from the page. The images of the day crowded brilliant and clamouring before her: the boy with the trolley: a curve for his head leading to a diagonal for his outstretched arm and the handle continuing on down to the box, horizontal and the wheels. She turned the page. She drew a tree, all angles and a scribble of defeated foliage; the handle of the well and its curved wall and a figure pressing down; a turban leading to a thin neck and out along a bent shoulder. She drew and drew with her eyes shut until her head drooped and the pencil struck her in the forehead. Then she lay back, holding the pad in one hand, forgetting everything, all memory reduced to shapes in the prolific dark. Towards dawn, she slept.

The pattern of the days that followed was set. She did a little work in the fields, helped with household chores when allowed, bought beer for herself and Chengue and the girls but hardly ever for Nathalie who contrived to be absent, always busy. Seán sometimes took food with them, more often not. His evenings were taken up with visits to neighbouring villages to confer with the elders about water supplies. Their wells were drying up too and the ferrying of water was a shared process. Women did not go to these meetings. On days when the clinic was being built, she tried to help, then sat in the shade, fanning herself with a bunch of withered brushwood twigs and watched.

At night the ritual wash and massage had become perfunctory. Water was provided and always for Birgit first, the pot of cream was opened for her and only once did Zizi and Amalia comb and plait her hair, giving her discreet glances of sympathy as Nathalie turned a silent profile and gave all her attention to a maths book. Enervated by the heat, the impassive clockwork dictations of the climate and the unimpeachable politeness of her hostesses, she gave up her search for opportunities to speak to Nathalie, sensed that the bond of language had been deliberately undermined. Small phrases, all formal, spoken in soft and courteous tones, were all that were offered. Chengue's outbursts at Zizi and Amalia were tolerable, understandable when compared to the focused absence of Nathalie's words and, to Birgit, harmless, an almost welcome sign that some aspects of their lives continued as normal.
In the morning of the sixth day as she sat tugging at the teat of a nerous piebald goat to get milk for the children, Seán arrived in

the jeep and came straight to where she crouched, willing the animal to trust her and trying to direct the white needles of milk into the gallon tin.

'It's come,' he said. 'Your suitcase. Delivered to the Excelsior Hotel. Five-star treatment after all.' The teats were warm, firmly crumpled in her hands as she frowned. She looked down at the bubbles circling in the little reservoir of milk, then stood up. The child who waited by her side put his two hands on the wire handle and eased the tin from her grasp and she watched him, running away with the tin held up to his chest.

That morning she had woken to the sound of Chengue and her daughters quietly rising, dressing, making breakfast. She had waited until they had gone outside and then had pulled the door open a few inches, to make her own small dawn. In the narrow cone of light she was surprised to see her jacket, t-shirt and jeans, newly clean and neatly folded in a pyramid at the foot of her bedroll.

Seán was animated, full of plans. Another consignment of water was on its way but would not arrive until the following morning, and meanwhile she and he could collect her case and have a night on the town. He would pay a visit to the bureaucrats, shake them up a bit. She looked at him and listened. What a quaint way he had of talking. Skimming along in diverting curves and yet finding the exact words, if one took the care to single them out. She looked at the pockmarks made by drops of milk that came from the udder, dark holes in the dust.

Calmly she said, 'I'll get my things.'

She took the goat back to its herd, holding its fibrous collar as the animal bobbed and ducked, anxious to be again with its own kind. In the hut she took off the wrap and folded it on the floor. She stepped into her own clothes and put her drawing pad in the pocket. After a long moment she took several notes from her wallet and put them under the jar of balm. She stopped at the door, looking back again at the orderly space, the perfect round containment of it, each thing mute in an arrangement that expressed a known order. She pulled her pad from her pocket and scribbled a note: 'Dear Nathalie, If I knew of any other way to thank you, I would –'

Would what? Make it? Do it? Words failed her. She folded the sheet and placed it under the money, then she went out and closed the door.

Seán had turned the jeep and was waiting with the engine ticking as he talked to Charlie where he stood on the running-board, one arm hooked about the wing mirror. Birgit looked around the village but neither Nathalie nor Chengue was to be seen and in the end she did not say goodbye, merely shaking Charlie's hand and smiling at him as she climbed into the passenger seat and fastened her belt for the long journey.

As the jeep ploughed along the track and then the smaller roads that led to the main highway to the capital, there was no comfortable moment in which to speak. When they reached the tarmacadamed motorway, the traffic thickened, flowing from tributaries until they entered the city on a fully roaring tide of vehicles.

Seán had left her at the doors of the Excelsior, and driven off to the Ministry for Rural Advancement. They had passed it on their way, a tall shabby building, studded with name-plates, like medals on a uniform, peaked awnings shading the narrow slots of windows. She wondered how he would be received and what he would use to soothe the nerves of the officials. He had a way of not appearing to be receptive. On the journey he drove with a speed and accuracy that seemed to deny doubt or hesitation. The bureaucrats would strive for answers.

She collected her case at the reception desk where a girl, slender and shiny as an eel, received her payment without a flicker, looking past her to a group of Asian visitors who were forming a mute queue. In the centre of the foyer was a fountain. She sat on the brink in the chill spray of droplets, fine as powder. She looked at the water jostling upwards, splurging down, flexing out, sidling in again to the centre in a continuous self-serving flow. Men in dark suits and tasselled loafers strode past in pairs, clasping briefcases. One glanced at her without turning his head. Had she spoken?

The hotel gift-shop sold pottery, small carvings, jewellery and scarves. She chose a square fringed stole for Margaret and for Jerome an ornate pipe. For her grandmother she bought a narrow band of mother-of-pearl, greenish, like her grandfather's pen, and a matching pair of earrings. Then she walked through the open glass doors to the taxi-rank at the kerb.

Seán was standing on the steps of the Ministry buildings, holding a straw hat with a wide brim in his hands, flapping it softly in front of him and scanning the street. As she stood on the lowest step and watched him run down towards her, she had a momentary sense that this was something she should remember, with the blue of the sky behind his head. He held out the hat to her.

They went to a restaurant on a side street where the shadows of the tall buildings and the lack of traffic offered a small measure of peace. The tables were widely spaced, the conversation of diners muffled by plants. Birgit hung her hat on the back of her chair and they sat facing one another at a small table. A waitress brought two menus. Birgit looked across at Seán.

'How was your visit to the Ministry?'

He made a balancing movement with his hand. 'Mm. We'll see. I had the element of surprise but ... Anyway I won't worry about it now. We're not going to talk about work, are we?' His voice was quiet and she waited for him to continue but he just looked back at her, all animation gone.

The waitress returned. She nodded cheerfully, 'Some wine while you decide?'

She brought a bottle of pale green wine and waited for them to taste it but Seán said, 'I'm sure it's fine, thank you.' He held his glass by its base on the table. Birgit put out her hand to touch his. The voice of a woman near the window could be heard laughing. A party of four got up and wandered out, paying their bill and chatting. One of the women readjusted a turquoise pin in her hair.

'Seán, I can't stay.'

He glanced at her and then muttered, 'I was afraid it might be something like that.'

'How did you know?'

'You've been so quiet.'

'I was trying to think of a way to tell you.'

He made a brief grimace. 'I was trying to think of a way of stopping you. What do I have to say to persuade you that you're needed?'

'By you? Seán –' She took her hand away.

'Of course by me.' His eyes darkened. 'You could teach, you could do translation work.'

'Seán –'

'This is about where you fit in, isn't it? Aren't those things you could do?'

The waitress approached the table, stopped and looked at them, then moved noiselessly away.

'It's not about me, no.'

'What was it then, a whim?'

'Of course not,' she snapped, then as he avoided her eye, she took a deep breath and rubbed her forehead. 'Remember at Christmas, all those wonderful stories, legends you told me, the fascinating picture you painted of life here? I had to see for myself – so when I got the opportunity, of course I took it.'

'But now you're sorry you did.'

'No. I'm glad I came.'

He had lifted the edge of the lace mat under the vase of flowers and was scrutinizing the filigree of stitches, tracing the fine pattern of curves.

'Then stay here.'

'I can't stay because I can't give my life to this place and nothing less will do.'

'You make it sound like a death sentence.'

She tried again, 'You have a deep feeling for this place.'

'And you are just skimming in and out like a –'

'A tourist? Was that the word, Seán?' She flushed and became pale.

He faltered, frustrated by the way some words splintered and fell, useless, while others hit false targets with such accuracy, belittling her intentions and herself.

He looked down at the table, at the wine, at the cloth, at the flowers, wanting those harmless props to become vital prompts. Then he turned his head aside.

She put out her hand and touched his again; a light nervous touch. In the quietest of voices she asked, 'What do you want me to say? That this is perfect somehow, that this is what I have always wanted, better than real life, or just better than what was before?'

The warmth of her hand on his reminded him of how easily their bodies had spoken to one another. 'Stay for me,' he wanted to say but the neat division beween work and play in his life had been too well achieved, it would not be undone instantly or at will.

As they left the restaurant the waitress picked up the tip, rolled it into a tight tube and poked it above her ear, into her scarf, then swept up the glasses and bottle in one neat movement.

On the way to the airport they did not speak, thinking of the gap that would soon be between them, like those distances which they had ignored, or simply, until now, not seen. She gave him the camera which she had in an uninspired moment bought for him, finding nothing suitable. He took her photograph while she attempted to smile, and then asked a passer-by to take a photograph of them together, and stood beside her while the amused man gestured to them to draw closer. Birgit put her arm around his waist and Seán laid his across her shoulders. Behind them the planes were inert, pampered deities being cossetted and groomed by scurrying acolytes.

He took back the camera and turned to her.

'Why did you come?'

'To see. To learn. To find out what it is about this place that brought you – that keeps you.'

'And? What did you learn?'

She frowned. 'That you are ... damn. My damn language leaves me just as I need it most. But wait, I have it: you are vocated.'

Through his misery a bead of amusement shone. The P.A. issued a string of sounds like an adenoidal muezzin. He glanced up at the speaker and then at her.

There was no one on the seat beside her, and as she looked out of the window at the familiar paraphernalia of the airport she wished that the preliminary checks would soon be over. At last the doors closed on the pungent air and the plane turned and started to move and she felt the acceleration's urgent pull until the machine tore itself away and rose like cream above the runway. The click of safety belts interrupted her from her daze and she saw in the window a reflected movement. A steward bent towards her, reached into the trolley and brought out a white cloth. She heard the muffled squeaks of the trolley continuing on its way as she unfolded the thin towel and pressed it to her face, inhaling its cool perfume and wondering at the kindness of strangers.

When she looked out of the window again, she could see nothing. She switched off the overhead light and leaned towards the glass, willing some image or shape to reach her. And still she saw nothing but the dark. She thought of the village, imagining it below, receding, until the small clusters of thatched cones became freckles on the dust. She saw the drops of goat's milk, the fan of withered scrubwood, the line of cloud on the horizon.

14

Inis Breac

The strangest thing, dear Oma, I was looking for
something in the pocket of my linen jacket and
found three postcards, written by me it seems,
when I was travelling back. They are such odd
things, not addressed to anyone, forlorn ramblings,
like a teenage diary, self-conscious. I think I can
remember buying them in some terminal. One has
a picture of a water tower. Another shows an aeroplane, as if to send a picture of an aeroplane somehow proved that I was in the air. The third showed
municipal gardens, you know those regimental beds
full of identical flowers, identically spaced, that
proclaim that nature, that nasty creature, is at last
under control. But if the pictures were strange, the
messages I wrote were even stranger. A mixture of
self-pity and tiredness. I cannot excuse them but I
am so very glad I did not send them. The little furnace of my stove has gobbled them contemptu-
ously, after all, it has already fed on so many failed
paintings, what are a few cards blurred with self-

pity? Do you know my luggage went astray? Now I almost imagine that it was my luggage that made the real journey, found its destination, had a perfectly pleasant visit and rejoined me, gratified, rejuvenated, and I was the shabby desertee, revolving on some surreal carousel at a speed that flung my senses into disorder.

And yet, not so, or not only so. In another pocket I found my drawing pad. It smelled of smoke and cooking oil, insect repellent, that thick balm that kept the flies away and prevented my skin from scorching. The pages had begun to warp and stick together. I could not sleep sometimes in that little hut that I shared with Nathalie and her family (that *they* shared with me), where the only sound was of breathing. I have one drawing: an abstract, five lines in waves that in the dark I saw, or imagined, as coloured. On the white page, they are five grey lines that could mean nothing to anyone but me.

I am sending you a drawing of a woman winding the handle to bring up a bucket from the well. That well, I can still see it, the centre of the village, always surrounded by women waiting their turn to try to coax a cupful of muddy water from its depths, their talk accompanied by the nervy whinge of the bucket being cranked up by those thin muscular arms that went up and down with the windlass handle. It was like some sulking god that had to have a host of supplicants, bending and straightening, bending and straightening, as if bowing to the metallic mantra which, from the shade of the hut where I sat making an artificial breeze with a brushwood fan, made it sound as though water was gold being ground from rock. (I must see to my stove, my own diminutive household god which roars with pleasure when I open its square door and make it an offering of sticks.)

What have I written? Hmm. Not a mention of Seán. It is strange how a sudden change, so great a change affects memory. When I was away, Inis Breac and the people I know here seemed almost eliminated. When I concentrated on them I found it difficult to remember even the most ordinary details and then, when I was not thinking or trying to remember, whole scenes would appear, like when I was in the shop, or when the hands of the women weeding brought a close-up picture of Margaret at her sink. And now (yes, I'm coming to it), when I try to think of Seán, he is so difficult to frame clearly. He seems part of that place, that unreal place, whose reality, when I was there, was relentless, inescapable. He wanted me to stay, which shows how little thought he had given it. I would not ask him to stay here. What would he do? Watch the rain squandered down the paths and boreens or see it decorate the windowpanes while I fight my selfish fight with pencils and brushes?

If I were to move all those thousands of miles, I would have to live in the village, and I would have to be useful, to work, to contribute something. I could not bear to be there without being useful. Even having a vocation (which I don't) might not be enough. I would always be taking more than I gave.

(You'll believe that – I haven't yet said 'thank you' for the most extraordinary week.) You will not say the obvious: that I am not useful here. My small rent is probably not needed and my friendship, would it be missed?

Margaret was very glad to see me. Even Jerome and Shep made a big welcome. I cannot imagine the island without them. I am here for selfish reasons and that I knew when I came.

I want to try to turn some of my sketches into paintings and I shall start with colour. And so, I need again, more paint. I have to go to town again anyway because I had a card from Seán's aunt, asking me to see someone. I was cold, almost numb when I came back, two days ago, but now, I find this winter full of energy.

Write soon and tell me about your holiday, your very different holiday.

Love, Birgit.

At the café, Birgit found a window-seat and sat with her coffee, looking across the road to where the antique shop and bookshop seemed held together in a bland conspiracy. She had read the notices in the windows and compared them. If the effect was the same, the way in which it was presented was quite different. The furniture and glass, clocks and paintings, made an enticing backdrop to the message in jaunty handwriting. The bookshop offered nothing, blinds on window and door concealed contents and interior and the note, on a torn envelope, was like a dismissal.

She opened the paper bag from the stationer's and took out a plain card. 'I have waited for an hour (a pleasant hour at the café), and knocked twice, I must go to catch the ferry. I shall be in town again soon but if you want to visit me at Inis Breac,' she paused, then with some reluctance wrote, 'you will be welcome at any time.' There would be no point in a half-hearted invitation, he was a shy man, he would need encouragement and yet she hoped that he might not come. If work was going well, she would not want to be interrupted. If it was going badly she would be in no mood to welcome an awkward acquaintance. Shame-faced, she underlined the word 'any' and crossed the road to put the card in the letter box.

An old man was passing by, using his stick to test the pavement for soundness before each step. He stopped and looked at her.

'You live here?' she asked.

He pointed with the stick, 'Up past the church.'

'Is the bookseller at home?' It sounded foolish. 'I cannot find him and I have tried more than once.'

'He's away, I'd say. The shop is closed always.'

'Ah.' She stepped back and looked up at the first-floor window, for want of something to do, then, nodding her thanks, she set off down the road, while the old man looked after her, glad of an excuse to stop and rest.

She unrolled the sheets of heavy paper and flattened them, then taking a pale fawn one, she lined up her new paints, the dark reds and browns, the oranges and ochres, and after pencilling in a background of huts and clusters of figures, she chose a new brush and took a deep breath.

She painted Charlie seated on the ground, his legs straight out, his head bent over pliers and a Coca-Cola bottle. On another sheet she painted a row of women walking to the fields in single file against a sun that had melted all colour from the sky. She put in the figures of children and goats, men leaning against the wall of the shop. On the fawn background, the colours were deep and rich. She took another sheet and painted the women at the well. On another she showed the builders at the clinic, on another, a man in a waterhole stretching up to put his basin of water on the ground. She covered sheets and sheets, in the light of the lamps. She pinned them up around the room to dry, as she went, more interested now in putting down everything she had seen, to make a living history rather than solve technical problems. She forgot her lack of skill and when she ran out of coloured paper, she found it was past midnight and she was ready to fall from tiredness.

15

He held the plain card in his hand and squinted until the moving lines congealed into legibility. Had he heard her knock? He glanced towards the street where twilight was thickening to the point that, at any second now, a motorist would turn on headlights and then night would pounce and windows like signals would light up to create a pleasanter day within the houses and night would retreat to the edges until much later. He dropped the card onto the pile on the table and went to switch on the overhead light, then picked it up again. The cards from Olivia and Jenny, with their blue skies and elegant statues, cathedrals and flower-framed seas, were littered on the table, glanced at and forgotten. The unadorned card from Birgit caught his attention. Somehow, it seemed to contain a threat or a command. He held it to his nose. No perfume, just ink on new card. The whiff of duty. Tangled handwriting, from one who had seemed so competent. He would have to do something to stave off whatever danger this presented. Phone messages had begun to accumulate. At first they referred to details: had they left the back window open? (Jenny); a poste restante for their mail (Jenny again); but Olivia always enquired about him and the last call had been almost cryptic, as though made surreptitiously, without Jenny's knowledge. She was worried that he never answered the phone: 'You wouldn't be just there, listening. You're not that sort of person. I suppose I'm imagining things. I'll just keep trying.'

The ring sometimes reached him in the insulated depths where, after a few drinks, he immersed himself willingly. By the time Birgit knocked, he had been at a different level again. As the line in the bottle lowered, it pleased him, the reliability of it, and he watched until, with his head on the table, the golden band narrowed so that he did not have to swivel his eyes upwards. Even that effort was spared. Then, knowing that there was an inch left in the bottle, he could sleep undisturbed, even by dreams. By a habit that had bided its time until it was needed again, he awoke each evening and, with the instant vigour contained in that last inch, he pulled himself up, out on his coat and slipped across to the off-licence, often hearing the imperious jingle of the evening news that held the street quiet for those few necessary minutes. Behind the counter, the proprietor gazed into the bar where the screen could be seen, high up, flashing its catalogue of disasters while he reached back to the spirits shelf behind him and rolled the bottle diagonally, with careless dexterity, in a sheet of newspaper. His wife sometimes took his place and she had tried to talk, but Geoff pretended not to hear and she soon gave up.

He drained the bottle, received its promised kick, and then tugged on the sleeves of his coat which hung from the chair where he was sitting, rose, took the empty bottle and stood it near the bin in the yard. The cat's dish had food in it, half eaten or rained upon, he could not make out which. He scraped out more and left the tin on the draining board with the spoon standing inside. He picked up the card again, hoping to find that he had been mistaken, but drew no comfort from it. An appearance was required: a proof, an assurance: some damn thing. He paused at the phone. If he waited, Olivia might ring again and then he could speak to her. If he could speak. 'Hello.' He heard the sound of his own voice escaping from some clogged and rusted engine, coarse, alarming. And as for plausible, soothing lies, they were beyond him. Olivia would only become more worried, would somehow contact Birgit, or Simon, even. He felt cold. He pulled his coat closer around him and left the house

The proprietor glanced at him as he asked for a naggin of whiskey and he stared back, discouraging enquiry. The bottle was wrapped and handed over without a word.

He leaned his back against the sink, unscrewed the cap and let it fall over his shoulder. It rattled in the metal bowl while he raised the bottle. 'Here's to one day of sobriety,' he said.

The nakedness of morning light revealed the interior of the house with unwelcome novelty. He had avoided it so well and with, he realized, such good reason. Neglect had become abuse: the chair with its back mysteriously broken, the raggedly disembowelled tins standing or lying on the draining board, the newspapers picked up, opened and then dropped, like heads of monstrous flowers, here and there, ashtrays, saucers, mugs and plates full of butts, like dirty little craters everywhere, and over everything a fine, uneven deposit of ash, like puffs of a dying volcano. The house had become the mirror he would not look into.

Fear slid down through him like a very fine wire. She must not see this. He found the card and pressed it against the table to steady his hand. If he did not find her she would find him and that would be worse but he had to have more to drink first and the whiskey, enough to warm and save him through the night, a short ration to wake him earlier, was finished. He bent the card and creased it. How easily his simple routine was destroyed. The off-licence would not be open. He looked at his watch. If he waited for it to open he would miss the ferry. He felt in his pocket and found the keys of the antique shop. He opened the street door and glanced up and down then quickly went next door and after a brief, furious tussle with the lock, opened the door. In the kitchen the decanter stood, smug and full as when he had last seen it. He held the stopper in one hand then raised the decanter, stopped and looked around. He found a glass, splashed port into it and raised it, grimacing at the smell, then gulped down the vile sweetness. He gagged and as he hastily poured another measure, hit the rim of the glass with the decanter. A bite-shaped sliver fell onto the counter. He held the decanter loosely to his chest as he picked up the broken crystal and tried to fit it back into its place. The piece fell into the glass, a hand-engraved goblet, very old. He stared then took one gulp from the decanter, spilling a little from its generous mouth and, as his system found the necessary fire, he planted the decanter back on the counter and replaced the stopper. He wangled the bolts back on the garden door and, taking the glass, flung it over the hedge into his own back yard.

On the ferry he sat in the bow, on the narrowest seat, at the farthest point from the ferryman, who was talking to the only other passenger, a man with a black leather bag. Neither was interested in talking to Geoff, who sank his head into his upturned collar and felt the light wind coolly lift the new growth of beard on his face. Fearful of catching sight of himself, he had done so by accident in a shop window and was relieved to see that the coat and beard were an effective camouflage.

The two men looked past him to the landing strip, where a tiny woman in a thick grey jumper, crossover apron and wellingtons was waiting. She had her hands clasped tight in front of her and as the boat came alongside she held them out, still tightly gripped in a gesture that was somewhere between a prayer and a greeting. The other passenger stepped ashore and put his arm around her and she talked up into his face. They moved away up the slip and the ferryman turned off the engine. 'The doctor will see him right,' he said, watching them. In the sudden silence her voice came back to them, a monologue of worry, no single word distinguishable. Geoff put three coins on the seat before the ferryman.

'Five o'clock, I'll be going out again,' said the ferryman.

Geoff stumbled ashore then steadied himself.

'Still not got your sea legs.'

'I – no. I wonder could you direct me?'

The ferryman paused with a coil of rope, a moving oval, draped from his hand.

Of course he couldn't remember her surname, or even if he had ever heard it. He cleared his throat. 'Birgit.'

'Bridget? She's that way.' He pointed. 'Beyond the three beaches. The last house, when you can go no farther. She's on the island today.'

At the third beach he realized he had already seen her house, that first day when he and the boys were exploring. He saw its chimney and a portion of the roof appear above the rocks, then the gable with a small window towards one side. She might be able to see him. He lowered his head, slowed his steps and buried his fists deeper in his pockets. Hands closed on nothing. He came offering nothing and had no idea of what he would say. The impulse to find her had been sparked by a fear of discovery. In his rush to fend off intrusion, he had failed to prepare himself. He plodded on, bereft even of the idea of retreat.

The cottage was empty. He knocked and waited, knocked again, opened the door and called 'Hello!', a cracked bark of sound that must have startled her, if she had been there. He went in, saw the chair near the stove and knew that tiredness would overwhelm him if he sat down. He backed away from the warmth and pulled the door shut behind him.

The sea had become a resolute, brilliant grey, a solid metal, and the cold made his face ache. The ferry would not go for more than two hours. He started to walk back along the path until he came to the hill that he had climbed with Stevie on his shoulders. It should be easier to climb unburdened but he felt a downward pull as if the hill had a magnetic core. At the top, he stood gasping and lit a cigarette to ease the wrenching of cold air on his lungs. A few goats strayed among the gorse below on the south side of the island where the slope of the hill ended above a strip of shingle that stopped suddenly at a wall of rock. In its shelter a figure crouched. He stared, putting his hand over his eyes against the low sun. It must be Birgit with a book on her knee, drawing or reading. He was unable to see her hand but her attitude was one of purest concentration on something beyond the book, on the ground near her feet. He watched for a time but she hardly moved. Surely she would have finished by the time he got to her. She might even finish at any moment and stand up and walk towards him, or walk away. He started to scramble down the hill, tripping and sliding, keeping his balance by luck more than skill as he watched her, fixing her in his gaze in case she would be gone and more energy, energy that he could not create, would be needed to find her again.

The shingle fell sharply to the water's edge and he struggled across it, his feet sinking in the wet pebbles and shells, his breathing harsh and painful. Suddenly she saw him and stood upright. He stopped a few feet from her, panting, a slime of sweat beginning to slide down his forehead, his breath tearing noisily at his lungs.

'Is it Mr, um, Geoff?' She frowned. Her alarm dwindled to puzzlement.

He looked down, embarrassed, and saw what she had been drawing. The triangular chunks of vertebrae, the twin loops of rib-cage, the skull lost in a tangle of seaweed, the huddle of slender arms and legs: the white, white bones of a very small child. He stood for a moment, holding his breath, then he folded down onto his knees and began to cry. The strangled sobs and gasps became louder, forced out by relentless pain. He repeated a word that she could not catch. Bending over him she could see the back of his neck, red and seamed, below the matted clumps of hair. She put her arm around his shoulder.

'What d'you say? What is it?' She leaned her head close to his face, trying to catch the word. He said it again and again. 'Rosie. Rosie drowned.'

'What is Rosie?'

'Rosie, my daughter,' he said, angry now. 'Rosie and Clare. My daughter, my wife. They drowned. They drowned. They drowned,' he shouted, wrenching himself around to stare at her through the flecked and smeared lenses of his glasses. He bent forward again, groaning and clasping his head between his arms.

'What?' She looked around and out to the empty sea. 'When?' She sensed a confusion but could not place it.

'Nearly twenty years,' he mumbled.

'Please,' she sat back on her heels and looked at the shuddering form. 'Let me help.' She put her arms firmly around him.

'I can see her now.' He raised his head and wiped his face with his hand. 'Sitting in the back seat, when they brought the car up. Her mother was still in the front. She'd been turning the car. We could see them from the shop where we were waiting for the ice-creams, Simon and me. It was there and then it was gone and ...' He took several gulps of air. 'When they brought it up, Clare had ...' his voice went into a broken caw, 'all ... her nails torn, from trying the window or the door, but Rosie was where she had been, in the back, holding on to the top of her mother's seat with both hands.' He swayed and Birgit propped him up, trying to make comforting sounds through his sobs.

He looked down at the bones. 'What is it?'

'A seal. A young seal, see?' She laid her hand at one of the wrists, 'Too long.' The fine bones protruded beyond her fingertips. She pushed aside the seaweed to show the skull tapered to a snout.

He grew quite still then shivered.

She looked into his blinded face, then took off his glasses and wiped them with the cuff of her shirt. She supported him and he leaned upon her without another word as they moved between land and sea on the ocean's unreliable edge.

The room smelled of paint as Geoff stood again near the stove and Birgit slipped his overcoat from his unresisting arms. He lay in the warmth of the chair with his hands trailing almost to the floor. She took the kettle from the hotplate and poured steaming water into a basin. She knelt beside him and washed his face with a soft cloth, dipping it into the water and rinsing it often. She washed his glasses and dried them and put them into his hand, then rested his hand on his lap. He closed his eyes and his breathing became shallow and peaceful. As she watched, he slept.

She sat at the table and looked at him. His head gradually sank onto his chest. The exposed eyelids looked soft: pouches accustomed to the shelter of glasses. The lines on his face ran down and disappeared into the beard. The lines of his arms, body and legs too all tended downwards. If she gazed much longer, she might imagine that he would slide into the ground and disappear. A pencil lay under her hand. Still looking at Geoff, she turned over one of the drawings on the table and began to sketch. How mysteriously the sleeper retreats into himself: the boiling tide overflows and then drains away: the sleeper becomes the flotsam of his own waking self.

She sketched more and faster. The lines began to converge and the form of the unconscious man grew strong on the page. Then the light died and she stopped. This was no night drawing coming free through the dark and she did not want to alter whatever had gone onto the paper. Eventually he stirred, said something and threw out his arm. The glasses fell to the floor and he woke, struggling upwards in the chair. She took his hand and turned on a lamp at the table. He looked at the cone of light, then at her and then around the room.

'Could you eat?'

He shook his head.

'Something to drink?'

Again he shook his head.

She put him in her bed, untying his shoes and drawing the woollen blankets carefully up over his chest. She sat on the end of the bed until his eyes closed again. All night she watched him, soothing him when he cried out, waiting when he twisted to settle the clothes on him again. When she held his hand it was like holding a set of bones, lifeless, linked together out of habit. The cold drove her to find her coat and shawl and, wrapped in them, she lay on the foot of the bed, curved around his feet, and dozed. Just before the darkness thinned, she fell into a fractured sleep.

The next day, Geoff slept and woke, gazed silently past her and sometimes spoke, going over the drowning again and again. At each telling, she crouched or knelt by the bed, holding his hand, noting how it changed from cool and flaccid to hot and tremulous, and then to cold again.

In late morning, she lighted the fire and, while he slept, made soup. This she fed to him, and though he had refused it, when she put the spoon to his lips, he drank. In the afternoon he rose and went to the front door. She asked if he wanted to go for a walk but he shook his head and stood watching the sea, inhaling and listening, as if he were trying to know it as anyone else might. Then he sat by the stove and watched the sky, passively noting each change. Now and then he sighed. When she stirred in her chair he turned his head towards the sound and then looked at her. She pulled an old sketch pad from the drawer of the table and turned it to show the blank backs of the pages.

'May I?'

He saw the poised pencil. A dim spark showed behind the lenses as he nodded. While she drew he watched her hand, sometimes met her look, then returned to watching the sky.

She found it difficult. The plumbline of despair had gone and, with it, many of the fine lines that in her first portrait had been so clear. After a time he said, 'I'll just snooze, if that's all right,' and while she still smiled at this formal politeness, he took off his glasses and closed his eyes. Immediately a vulnerable look returned, but this time it was peaceful, the equable exposure of one who felt at ease.

16

The queue at the Country Market was at a standstill. People assumed attitudes of professional patience, balancing baskets on hips, gazing at the high beamed ceiling of the church hall, chatting to one another over armfuls of scrawny thinnings and sprays of winter-flowering shrubs. Some lodged the baskets on the floor, preparing to push them forward with a foot, if the queue ever did move, while watching the cautious rovings of children in wellingtons and bobbled hats. Becky held out change to a woman who voiced long and expert opinions on the merits of redcurrant jam. She nodded and waited, the change growing warm in her palm. Her helper who had flicked open another plastic bag for the next customer, suddenly took the coins and said airily, 'Whose is this?' The redcurrant expert took her change and the hint and moved on.

'Bet *you* haven't all day,' said the helper to the woman from the off-licence who crashed her baskets gratefully onto the table. They unloaded potatoes and turnips, jars of preserves and earthy parsnips.

'Mrs MacCarthy,' said Becky, 'how was Christmas?'

The well-tamed hair was under the control of four gold combs which gleamed as she nodded. 'Quiet, the way we like it.'

'The same as ourselves.' Becky turned to Simon, who leaned

against the door behind her.

'Cardboard box?'

'I was saying the same thing to your dad,' Mrs MacCarthy said absently as she directed the box-filling.

Simon stopped unfolding a flap and looked at Becky.

'One jamjar at each corner, for balance, like.' Mrs MacCarthy gave a half turn to each jar as though screwing it to the base. 'There we are now.'

'Let me carry it for you.' Simon swept up the box and marched ahead of her to the door where he stood back to let her through. She scuttled ahead, pointing, 'The blue one. That's me.' He put the box in the boot of her car and closed it.

'When did you last see him?'

'Oh, a couple of days ago, it must've been. Crossing the street?' She rooted for her keys and sat in. 'Thank you.'

'You'll have to go,' said Becky,

Simon bowed his head.

At the door of the bookshop, he stopped as the key engaged in the lock. He had a sense that if he quietly withdrew it and put it back in his pocket, he could avoid a catastrophe: the pin would be put back into the grenade before the clip was released. He opened the door.

The smell of cigarette smoke was heavy but he could not judge how stale. As the first breath caught in his throat, he stood, certain that the door to the kitchen would open and Geoff would stand there, in surprise, in dismay. The rattle of a blind, the rumble of a lorry in the street quenched the silence and his attempt to gauge it. He went slowly to the kitchen where the smell of fat burned onto the grill mixed with the aseptic stench of ashtrays and the headier aura of spirits. He saw the broken chair and the dish of cat food, dry now, but still making its own sinister undercurrent of decay. He pushed open the window, nudging the whiskey bottle that stood in the shadow of the sink. He went out into the yard and saw the crammed bin and the overflow of bottles. The cat eyed him from the top of the wall. The remains of fresh food were in another dish where a splash of red from a broken glass mingled with a trace of milk. Automatically, he picked up the pieces of glass and put them in the bin. Then he turned and stared down the weedy path to the river. Refusing to allow himself to think, he walked down to the bank and looked into the water. It appeared swollen and slow but he could not guess its depth.

He hurried back to the house and searched all the rooms. The bed was cold and unkempt. The sitting-room had the close air of an unused space. Taking a deep breath, he opened the bathroom door. The reflection of the door's edge moving in the cabinet mirror was the only sign of life. His own face, its pallor, startled him. The look in his eyes was not, could not be, of fear. He shut the door firmly and ran downstairs. He glanced at the yard again but not towards the river. He counted the bottles. One for each day since Christmas. He looked again. There was an empty bottle on the table, small, curved. What did they call it, that hip-flask shape?

Maybe the small bottle was the start and he'd graduated to full bottles of whiskey. Could that mean that he'd gone to the off-licence now and was at this moment watching Mrs MacCarthy seize another bottle between her scarlet claws and smother it in yesterday's paper?

At any moment the door would open and he'd lurch in, woozy and vague, bumbling and troubled, pathetic and rev-, but the word 'revolting' would not come. It was usurped by the insistence of another: rev- riv- : river. No. Impossible. Unthinkable.

He stood up. He would go to the off-licence, find Geoff there and make a huge scene. It would be a grand finale.

He fled into the bookshop and looked at the counter, riffling through the papers, kicking those that had been dropped on the floor, looking under the counter and along the shelves and, at last, towards the centre table. He found Birgit's card, read it, read it again and stuffed it into his pocket as he left the shop.

As he passed the off-licence, he could see Mrs MacCarthy, alone, absorbed in a magazine.

The last shoppers were leaving the market and Becky was reconciling the money, her head bent over the cash box, as she counted under her breath.

'Well?'

'Not there.'

'So he *is* gone away.' She sat up, her eyes shining.

'Well, he's not there now.'

'But,' she lowered her voice, 'he has been?'

He nodded. She sagged into her chair.

Simon came around the table and, sitting on it, blocked her from the room. He took her hand. 'He seems to have been on a bender.' He felt her hand tense in his. He squeezed it. 'There's this card.' He took it from his pocket. 'It's dated yesterday, so that's where he may, where he must be.'

'Will you go?'

He nodded.

'Go now. He –' She closed her lips. She had long given up saying 'he needs you'.

He had almost missed the ferry. He backed the car to a turning point on the track to make room for an ambulance that was parked end-on to the landing strip, pointing towards town.

'I wouldn't have waited,' said the ferryman, 'but there's no one on the other side yet.'

Simon looked across to the island, where there was no movement.

'Poor Jerome Donovan,' the ferryman patted the hood of the engine. 'He took a turn. But sure a few days in hospital and he'll be as right as rain.' The sky was cloudless, the water swayed silkily. He started the engine and the boat eased away from the slip. Words such as 'doctor' and 'phone' came singly above the noise but Simon caught very little and merely nodded from time to time, realizing that nothing more was wanted.

When they came to Inis Breac he stepped ashore and turned to say, 'Will you need any help?' The ferryman shook his head. 'Those ambulance lads are professionals, but thanks.' He sat down on the centre thwart to wait. Simon asked directions to Birgit's house. A gleam came into the ferryman's eye. 'Isn't she the popular girl!' he said.

At the top of the road that led up from the slip, Simon stopped. In the distance ahead he could see, outlined by the sun, a small procession: two men in donkey jackets with fluorescent safety belts, carrying a stretcher. Its weight gave their footsteps a formal rhythm. Behind them came a tiny figure, as small as a child but with the stilted walk of someone much older, weighted on one side by a bag, and last, trailing like a redundant shadow, the low shape of a dog.

He watched for a moment then turned left onto the narrow road that led to the three beaches. He distracted himself from the task ahead by trying to recall details of the September picnic. Or had it been in October? Blackberries and football and swimming: September, then. The ball smacking off the water and the dog, like a referee, changing direction constantly. And after the picnic, lying beside Becky, knowing that she was asleep, just, but that if he moved to follow Geoff and the boys, she would wake. He admired the way that she had never lost that new mother's ability to decode sound in her sleep, like soldiers who slept through shells and bombs but woke at the smallest noise resembling a footstep. To Becky, his relation to Geoff must have always seemed like a silent conflict, a war of nerves, the piling up of spent, wasted opportunities. He watched his feet plod, left-right, left-right, one in front of the other, through the tufts of quivering, sprightly grass. And now? He stopped and looked up. Blue smoke stood straight up from the chimney of the cottage.

He waited at the door for a moment, then took a breath, tapped, paused, then gently pushed it open. The kitchen was warm and crowded with paintings. The silence was made louder by the shift and rustle of the stove. How long would he have to wait? The back door was closed and the only other door firmly shut too. He could not search this house. Reluctantly, he sat at the table. Idly, he lifted the first sheet of paper: another painting, still not quite dry. Underneath was a drawing of a young woman, head and shoulders. She might have been beautiful but somehow the elements of her features did not come together. He turned it over incuriously. On the back was the finished drawing of an old man. He was slumped, his bearded chin sagging on his chest, his arms flopped by his sides. Lifeless, or dying. What kind of woman would sit there and calmly draw a man who was dying? The sad, bereft passivity of the body. Couldn't she have done something? He shook himself and let the drawing fall back onto the table. Perhaps it was not hers. Then who? Wasn't there a German who used to draw people on battlefields, in defeat? Dix. Otto Dix, that was it.

He heard the click and saw the latch move. He stood up.

'You must be Birgit,' he said, taking the card from his pocket, while she remained, startled, in the doorway, holding a drawing pad under her arm. He ran his hand through his hair as she glanced at the card. 'I'm so sorry. I need to know if he's, if he, I'm –'

'You're his son.' She came into the room. 'He mentioned your name, I think, Simon? But you look so like him.' She was just beginning to be at ease but then she looked down at the table. 'Oh, you found the drawing.' She was looking at the portrait of the man.

'This? Oh, yes. It's umm,' he became silent.

She looked puzzled. She put her hand on the back of a chair at the other side of the table and said, 'You can't see the resemblance?'

He picked up the drawing and sank into his seat.

'This? This is *him*?'

The long silence was unbroken. Finally he said in a whisper, 'But what has happened to him?' He looked up at her, hardly able to see her against the light. 'Where is he?'

'He is here.' She moved her head slightly in the direction of the closed door. 'He is sleeping. He must rest. He got up for a while yesterday and seemed a little better but then he went back to bed. We must not wake him.' She moved her hands in a slow circular gesture. 'He is, I don't know what. I found him. No. No, he found me, on the shore where I was sketching. He was wild, incoherent.'

'Drunk?' said Simon.

'No, no. He was –' she searched for a word. 'Destroyed? Distracted? And then he saw the skeleton and he just collapsed.'

Simon's white face seemed to contract. 'Skeleton?'

'Oh, just a small seal. The sea uncovers things now and again. But he thought it was a child. He said something about a car.' She became silent.

Simon looked away from her. In an aloof voice he said, 'My mother and sister.'

'I'm so sorry.'

'It was a long time ago. I can think about them.' He sighed

and swallowed then turned his eyes towards the drawing. He covered the figure with his arm and hand, then splayed out his fingers to catch reluctant glimpses of the face. 'No glasses,' he said, then sniffed, rubbed his forehead and made a grimace. Then he sat up, leaned back in his chair and looked at Birgit.

'I am sorry,' she said again. 'The drawing –'

He shook his head. 'No. It is not you who has brought him to this.' He became absorbed in it again.

In the silence, Birgit looked around. Inspiration failing she said, embarrassed, 'Do you want ... would you like, perhaps tea?'

He shook his head. 'Thanks.'

'Then shall I see if he is awake?'

He barely nodded.

She opened the door of the inner room silently and stood with her hand on the knob. Greyish light behind the closed curtains made a pearly halo that dissolved the edge of her profile. There was no sound from the bedroom. She came back leaving the door ajar. 'I think he is waking,' she whispered.

Simon pressed his hands on the table and forced himself up out of his chair. As if she had not been there, he walked past her.

The light in the bedroom was of powdered silver. It rested softly on his father's face and beard, muting the colour of his hair and skin. His hands lay neatly on the quilted counterpane, translucent and still. He opened his eyes and looked at Simon. Then he turned over one hand and opened out the fingers, making a hollow of his palm.

17

Dear Oma,

So many things are happening, I can hardly count them myself, or account for them to you. I am sure you want to hear something more, well, something more coherent about Africa, but such a strange thing happened yesterday.

I was on the shore, on a part of the island that I don't see very often. There are no houses there, so no paths and the hill down to it is covered in bracken and briars and some gorse, terrible when alive but even more savage when it is dead. Covered in brilliant yellow flowers most of the year, like warning lights, but not now. I had been trying to draw Nathalie. Have I mentioned her to you? She is a teacher whose hut I lived in with her and her mother and sisters. She is very beautiful and so, you might think, an obvious person to draw but though I had made many paintings of the village and all the people at work or just resting, somehow, she was not in them. She holds her classes for all the children of the village in the shade of a big tree. She is very important in the life of the place (she teaches adults at night, reading, writing, maths) but I managed to leave her out. In one way she was my best friend there, and yet I lost her almost as soon as I had found her. She rescued me when I arrived, shaken to pieces by the bus, suffocated by dust, exhausted from too little, too bad, sleep, and 'dying' of thirst. (Oh how we dramatize ourselves! And yet I felt as though thirst had become a huge mouth that was swallowing me.) I wore her lovely robes that smelled of earth and plants; she made me a turban and soothed my skin with ointment. It was like being reborn, that first day, but then it all changed. It changed from the time Seán arrived. From that moment she began to withdraw and I never reached her again. She became a polite stranger. There was no falling out, only the slow realization that I had caused a disturbance, upset some balance, distorted a delicate fabric. Seán seemed unaware of it. So now you can see why I have not written so much about her. But she has come right up through my memory as sharply as the daffodil blades point up through the grass outside my window. I had been trying to draw her and had failed. The features all seemed correct, as I remembered them, but they did not cohere into a portrait. They were like an identikit picture: a collection of unrelated parts that had been assembled without, without what? An emotional centre? An aesthetic unity (whatever that might be)? Something more obvious, the presence of the subject? I realized that I have not the skill to make a drawing without a sitter. In disappointment I put my sketch pad in my pocket and went out to the shore.

There were storms while I was away. The edge of land and sea is a treasure trove at such a time as this. And I was rewarded: the bones of a seal pup, buried in the shingle on the south side of the island, were uncovered. The wind there rages in, unstopped from the ocean and roots about like someone in great haste, trying to find something in a trunk and then going off again suddenly, leaving everything disturbed, some things broken and others newly found. Those little bones were such an easy subject, full of shapes and angles, and the way they lay, so expressively curved, so recognizable. But the man didn't recognize them. He appeared, dragging his feet in the soft shingle, hair wild, in fact all of him wild, demented. I got a fright, such a fright, and I didn't recognize him at first. When he saw the bones, he fell down on his knees and cried: a dreadful sound. It was only a few weeks since we had met for dinner on Christmas Eve, but somehow he had disintegrated. His wife and daughter drowned in an accident. He talked as if he could see it still, no, as if he were seeing it happen just then and not twenty years ago. You might think he sounds mad but he did not mistake the bones for his daughter. He thought they were of some small child. When he realized what they were, he lost all interest in them and I was able to bring him home. And though he was sad and exhausted, he was no longer wild.

His son came and took him away today after two nights at my house. And that is everything.

Well, not quite everything. When his son came, I was out. I had gone down to the shore to find my pad which I'd dropped and then forgotten and when I came back, Simon was sitting in the kitchen, looking at a drawing I had made of his father while he was asleep. I had been trying to make a drawing of Nathalie, before all this happened, and it had gone so wrong. Then when Geoff was resting in the chair, I looked at him, looked and looked and my worry and fear for him began to disappear because he was calm, sleeping. And I became fascinated with his appearance. He was at ease and I think people who are having their portraits made are never at ease, so it was irresistible and I found myself sketching, trying to get those lines which read almost like signs: 'Here is a man who wants to sink down into the earth', 'Here is a man abandoned'. Those come to me now but then I was just wholly fixed on capturing a good subject. I suppose I did my best to comfort him and yes, he was comforted but still, I did the drawing. I didn't want him to see it and then when Simon found it, I was ashamed. But, fool that I am, I had to tell him that it was of his father because he hadn't recognized him. What a lot of not recognizing things/people. D'you suppose that we, any of us, know who we really are? This reads like a confession. I am afraid I have taken the sorrow of a man felled by grief and used it to extend my own morsel of talent. And yet it is the best thing I have drawn, so much better than the later sketches I made of him the next day, when he was starting to recover. He knew I was drawing him then and did not mind. He was even a little bit amused. But his face had become softer, younger, the wrinkles smoothing out, the hollows filling, even a faint colour coming into his skin, that harsh edge (so much easier to draw) gone. As though he found he was being looked at closely and (I admit it) admired. Now if only *those* drawings were anything as good as the first! What d'you think?

And now there is a knock on the door. You see? Everything happens at once!

Love, Birgit.

18

The doctor came downstairs followed by Simon. Becky, waiting in the kitchen, watched and held the teapot.

'Dr O'Brien?'

He hesitated and then put his bag on the floor.

'A cup would be nice. I'm at the end of my rounds anyway.'

He sat at the table and his bulk seemed to displace everything in the room as they waited for him to speak.

'I was saying to your husband, his poor father has been through the wars. And yet I couldn't find anything wrong with him.' He nodded and thought. 'He's had a bit of a shock.' He paused again, holding his mug on the table. Simon cleared his throat.

'He has something of a drink problem.'

'Ah.'

'Well, he had stopped, you know, for a couple of years but then he went on a spree recently.'

The doctor seemed interested in the dresser. 'Christmas is always a hard time,' he said quietly. 'And he's not so old, fifty-four, fifty-five? But that would account for it.' He turned to Becky. 'It's not that there's anything wrong as such but there's no go to him, is there?'

She looked unhappy.

'He was fine but now I think he's lost interest, hasn't he?' She looked to Simon who caught her eye then dropped his glance.

'That's about it,' he said.

'Well,' the doctor drained his mug, 'this'll help. Tonic and sleeping pills.' He scribbled briefly and put two prescriptions on the table, stood up and picked up his bag. He looked around.

'Ye have a lovely place here. And cosy. He'll be safe enough and the company'll do him good. Lives on his own?' He clasped his bag shut. Short gold hairs gleamed on the backs of his big square hands. 'Yes, the bit of company and a few decent meals.'

Simon coloured and Becky, looking stricken, went upstairs while he showed the doctor to his car.

Geoff lay in bed in the spare room where he had been since Simon had brought him home the previous day. The simplicity of the unused room with its pale blue bedspread and single chair made it look as though it had been prepared for an invalid. The bunch of haws, cheerful in a glass vase on the windowsill, only added to the sense that the room resembled a hospital. With spoons and bottles and packets of pills, it would only become worse. But when she sat on the edge of the bed he opened his eyes and said, 'I'm not ill, you know. There was no need to get' – he glanced towards the door – 'him. A doctor.'

'It was just a check-up. We were worried.'

'Sleep. I find it so hard to sleep. It keeps coming back to me.'

She wanted to calm him. She touched the turned-down edge of the sheet and started to speak but he was looking beyond her. She waited, wondering if it was the whiteness of the pillow that made him seem drained of colour. He frowned and looked at her again.

'I keep asking myself what I could have done. She was such a good driver but she was nervous, I knew she was nervous of piers. I could see the roof of the car still with the water and I jumped in and tried to open the door. Clare was calling, not screaming. You could tell she was in a panic but she was trying not to frighten Rosie. And I called back and said to hold on and we would get them out. There was another man. He was at the other side of the car but the doors would not open. Then there was a sudden movement, a subsidence, and the car went down. And I let go. I let them go.' He put his hands over his eyes. Becky stroked his arm and said, 'You did your best.'

'You don't understand. The other man dived but I just kept bobbing about on the surface like a bloody cork, no matter what I did. The cries got louder and then quieter and the thumping stopped. After that I can't remember what I did.' He took his hands from his eyes. 'But I keep seeing the roof of the car in the sun and then coming up from that filthy water and the two of them –' he caught his breath.

'You must stop tormenting yourself.'

'But I keep seeing it. It keeps coming back.'

Tom and Stevie had been apprehensive since they saw Geoff come slowly through the front door with Simon close behind him. They looked at his beard and his tangled hair and, when Becky had taken his coat, at his stained clothes and his nicotine-yellow fingers that shook. He had slowly eased himself onto the settle and avoided their eyes until Rex came up and nudged at his knees with his bony head in careless recognition and then Stevie had come up and leaned against him and timidly touched his beard saying, 'You're not a bit like Santa,' and then he had smiled.

Becky had hesitated but then she said, 'Granddad's not very well. He's going to stay with us until he's better.'

They watched, silent with wonder, as she put a mug of tea into his hands and held them until the shaking lessened.

After he had gone to bed Tom said, 'What's wrong with him?' Simon put down his knife and fork on the plate of food that he had been unable to eat and looked for help to Becky.

'He has bad dreams,' she said. 'He can't sleep. He needs us to mind him.'

This satisfied them and they had been quiet in the house, the next day, occasionally contemplating him from the doorway of the spare room, as he lay, neither awake nor asleep, held in the inexorable panorama of his memory.

After a couple of days he came downstairs. He was wearing an old pair of corduroys and a jumper of Simon's. Borrowed slippers and the fine trace of beard completed the picture of an elderly man. Becky looked at the obedient, listless way he ate his breakfast, putting the egg-spoon silently back on the saucer when he had finished, nodding silently when offered more tea.

'How did you sleep?'

'Like a stone. No more dreams. I suppose the pills fixed that.'

'That's good, isn't it? I mean, just for the moment?'

He was silent again and then he turned to her. 'I'm not keeping you awake, am I? Like I did the first night and you had to come in and ...'

'We both did. Simon was there too. We wanted to. We wanted to see that you were all right.' She did not say that his sleep was now so deep that she checked during the night, as she had done when the boys were newly born, to see if he was still breathing.

'Ah.'

That dream, where he dived down and reached the car and saw Clare's face, screaming now, but silently. He opened his mouth to say something and the water, thick black water, filled his throat and then he was drowning and Clare was still crying (he could see now), 'Help us! Help us!'

'Would you like to come for a walk?' Stevie was beside him. Becky started to say something and then stopped, seeing Simon in the doorway.

188

They walked to the end of the lane, past the pewter boles of the beech trees. Stevie held Geoff's hand and Simon walked on the other side, slowly, close to him. The child's hand was so small, so warm in his, it seemed to glow, a gentle, lively ember.

'That's Mr Holly's farm,' Simon was saying, pointing across the broad valley to a pink-washed house. Geoff felt his eyes brim with tears as he stared at the farm, afraid to blink. Simon glanced at him and stopped. 'Is there something the matter?' Stevie threw his head right back to see Geoff's face.

'It's the cold, I think. It makes my eyes water.'

'We'll go back.' Simon took his arm and the three of them wheeled about slowly as if practising the steps of a formal dance.

In the afternoon he sat by the fire, pretending to read the paper, seeing Simon's ten-year-old face perplexed between the ice-cream woman and a policeman. What was it he had said? 'You were gone so long I had to eat the other ice-cream,' and 'Why are you all wet? Why are you looking at me like that?' and 'Where are Mum and Rosie? What's happened to them?'

Simon appeared late in the afternoon with Tom and Rex. Tom chattered to Becky in the kitchen and Simon came across the room to lay something soft on his knee: the jumper that Olivia and Jenny had given him for Christmas.

'You have been in my house?' The thought appalled him.

'It's fine. Not to worry.'

'But –'

'And the cat, what's his name? Dundee? He's okay.'

Simon looked at him these days, but in small snatches, stray glances that did not linger. It was as though he was afraid that Geoff might disappear but was embarrassed to be caught looking at him so frequently.

'There were messages for you on your machine, from Olivia. And a number.'

'Oh?'

'I rang and said you were staying here. She seemed surprised. Sounded a bit scattered in fact.'

'Olivia?'

'No, her sister.'

'Jenny.' Geoff was puzzled. 'How is Olivia?'

'I'm not sure. It's all rather confused. Jenny didn't seem to know that Olivia had been phoning you so she wanted to know what you wanted and I had to say that there were messages asking for you. Nothing more.' Simon was standing at the window, running his fingers through his hair and looking directly at Geoff: an ordinary person, trying to explain something that he did not understand himself. 'You see,' he came and sat on the end of the sofa nearest to Geoff, 'it sounded as though her mind was completely elsewhere, as though I'd interrupted her. And then she suddenly said she had to go. So I said maybe when they had time they might ring you here and I gave her our number. I didn't think of saying I'd get you to ring them.' He looked apologetic.

'They're moving around,' Geoff said. 'There was nothing else you could have done.'

When he lay in bed that night he went over the conversation again and again. At last, they had found something else to talk about, something they could, together, be perplexed about. And when they had become silent, it had been the comfortable silence of commonplace doubt, not the chasm of the past, echoing with rage and sorrow. In the now familiar bedroom, the dark was a gauzy mobile accumulation of black dots which, as a child, he had imagined to be a tent, created by his parents to keep him safe during the night.

19

They sat in the mortuary chapel, a small building with a steep pitched roof and coloured glass windows that threw anaemic pinks and yellows on their clothes, making Margaret's Sunday best coat look black, though it was in reality dark red, and bringing a greenish tinge to Birgit's hair. The polished bench on which they sat, their backs to the wall, was at right angles to the coffin where Jerome lay, his hands folded on rosary beads. The padded lining with its frilled edge did not soften the austere lines of his forehead and profile. His skin gleamed and his expression was the familiar one, his natural reserve made permanent, or at least presented formally for his last appearance.

Margaret held on to Birgit's hand and stared at Jerome, sighing frequently. 'They'll be here any minute now,' she whispered, tightening her hold.

This apprehension of her family had been her recurring theme since she had arrived on Birgit's doorstep. Birgit had just finished writing to her grandmother and when Margaret burst out, 'He's gone!' she had glanced over her shoulder towards the beach, half wondering if it was Geoff who was the subject of Margaret's exclamation. Her hair had escaped from the bootlace that kept it locked on the back of her neck and her eyes blazed above cheeks where frazzled veins made red patches.

They went to Margaret's house, Margaret explaining loudly on the way how Jerome had been much better but that after lunch he had become agitated, calling for priests and lawyers but having to make do with herself as sole audience to his last wish: to be buried on Oileán Cré. She had agreed. 'What else?' she turned her burning eyes on Birgit, 'What else could I or anyone do?'

They took his suit from the wardrobe and folded it carefully between sheets of newspaper. They put his black shoes into the box that had come with them when they were bought. They compared his two ties and chose the plain green one because he had preferred it to the brown. There was no choice for the shirt: it was his only white one and could not in any case be bettered. And all the time Margaret talked about their relations: how much they resented the idea of Jerome's being buried outside of the plot in the town cemetery, how they had argued that it was strange, odd, the unhinged ramblings of a dying man, he couldn't know what he was saying, how they had even hinted that she might have dreamt this up herself and, seeing that this had only set her more firmly against them, they speculated that the island churchyard might be no longer consecrated as a burial ground. This was easily contradicted since Margaret, voluble in certainty, pointed out that she herself had attended the previous funeral there, not twelve months earlier. Having silenced them, she left, to return to Inis Breac for Jerome's clothes. Birgit began to understand the necessity for her presence and when the door to the mortuary opened, she held Margaret's hand tightly and they sat up very straight. When they were introduced, cousins and relations by marriage, nieces, nephews and their children, Birgit shook their hands and by her distracting presence, the avenues of argument were smoothly deflected.

A decade of the Rosary, led by the priest, was said. The pattern of the much repeated prayers became a tuneless drone. The mourners shuffled out and Margaret was left to make her last farewell before the lid of the coffin was set in place and screwed down. Birgit tried to leave but Margaret held on to her. When the door had been closed and the room was quiet, Margaret stood up and bowed her head. From her seat, Birgit could see her hair, tightly contained under a felt hat. She reached down and kissed Jerome on the forehead, put a dark-covered book beside him, let her hand rest lightly on his for a moment, then she turned to Birgit and said, 'We may as well go now.' The undertakers came forward from the shadows, then, as the lid was being moved over the coffin, one of them reached in and took out the book. Margaret snatched it from his hand and put it firmly back into the coffin.

'*The Voyages of Sinbad?*' said the undertaker.

''Twas his favourite book.'

The undertaker was dubious.

'And who was Saint Jerome if he wasn't the patron saint of books?'

They waited until the last screw was tight in place and then they turned their backs on the undertakers and went outside to where the rest of the mourners stood shifting their feet on the gravel and murmuring to one another in the cold.

Margaret's air of defiance carried her through the journey to the pier, where a few bystanders stared as the coffin was loaded onto the ferry and the small flotilla of boats left its moorings and headed out west for Oileán Cré. She ignored the expressions of relief on the faces of her relations as the well-kept slip and steps of concrete came in to view. On the crossing they had held their headscarves and hats and clutched their children (those who had not been quietly detached from the cortège before it left the chapel) with the grim attitudes of emigrants facing unknown hazards. The men shouldered the coffin from the ferry which had beached straight onto the strand just below the churchyard and pretended not to notice the water that would leave white salt-marks on the leather of their shoes. The priest ignored the sense of levity that spead among the mourners when the coffin-bearers staggered on the rough edge of the churchyard, trying to keep their footing, coffin and dignity in equilibrium. Even Margaret smiled.

Jerome was buried beside his parents. As the first crumbs of soil fell on the coffin, Margaret trembled and seemed about to break down, but when Birgit tightened her arm around the tiny woman's shoulders she drew in a deep breath and merely nodded, a slow, constant dipping of the head, as though burial, death and bereavement were a fulfilment of something that she could not, did not want to, deny.

The last of the neighbours had gone. The gilt-edged ware from the china cabinet had been carefully washed and piled up on the draining board. The remains of the ham had been scraped from the plates and thrown into the yard for Shep. Margaret and Birgit sat on either side of the fire in the kitchen, which still echoed to the sounds of voices. The relations, having survived one sea journey, had made the short crossing from Oileán Cré to Inis Breac almost cheerfully.

The calm weather that turned the waves into dark blue over-lapping plumes had banished the wind and only the motion of the boats gave an illusion of a breeze, lifting a scarf here and there as the Donovans and their families looked about them, covertly enjoying the outing.

After they had gone, the few neighbours lingered, reminiscing about Jerome, examining the medals that he had won in rowing regattas and estimating how many islanders were still living, in different parts of the world. No one cared to count how many, how few, were left on Inis Breac.

''Tis quiet,' Margaret said, 'but the summer won't be long in coming and then there'll be plenty of visitors.' She watched Birgit.

'Do they, your family, want you to move over to the mainland?' Birgit had become adept at finding the thread in oblique remarks.

Margaret sat up. 'Indeed they do but they may as well save themselves the bother. 'Twas the best thing Jerome ever did for me.'

'To be buried on Oileán Cré?'

Margaret nodded emphatically.

'We never moved. We were happy here from the first day. Why would we want to go anywhere and why would I want to move now?' It was almost a speech.

That was what had kept her going all day, that unexpected parting gift. She lay back in her chair, her eyes hollow now and her face very pale. Even the high-coloured cheeks had become a dull purple.

Birgit took the short-handled brush that stood by the fire and swept the ash neatly back under the grate. She filled the kettle and put it on the gas. She found a stray ashtray and emptied the butts into the fire, then she took a cloth and started to dry the dishes. At the sound, Margaret started up and began to protest. But Birgit came across the room and crouched by her chair saying, 'Please let me. And you rest, please.'

As she made careful piles of the plates, saucers, bowls and cups, she could see Margaret lying back, her head turned towards the fire, quite still.

In 'The Room' she arranged the ware very carefully in the cabinet and swung the door to, clipping the hook in the eyelet.

Frosted onto the glass was a pair of swans on a lake edged with bulrushes. She traced the picture with her fingertips, prolonging the moment, to give Margaret time to herself.

When she returned, Margaret was stuffing a damp ball of handkerchief up her sleeve. Birgit took the hot-water bottle from the hook above the sink, filled it and put it gently on Margaret's lap. Margaret looked up.

'Will you call to me tomorrow?'

'Of course.'

At the door Shep came to Birgit and nosed her hand. She patted him and he followed her for a few steps then looked back towards the house, then he slowly returned to the door and lay on the step.

January 25th

Dear Birgit,

I write to thank you for the money. I did not wish to keep it because you do not owe me. My mother found it while I was at school and she hid it, otherwise I would have sent it back to you. She went away to visit her cousin at a village many miles from here and when she was there she bought two pieces of land. Now Zizi and Amalia have dowries and soon they will have husbands.

Everything has changed here. The rains did not come and hungry people from other villages north of here are arriving every day. The government has set up a food distribution centre in the building that should have been the clinic. The children are becoming too hungry to learn, so I no longer teach. I help with the food but the supplies are very uncertain. Sometimes they get stolen on the way here. The government sends armed guards but they can cause a lot of trouble. Soon I shall have to go to the city for work as there is no money and so little food here. My mother may come with me or she may stay with my sisters. For the first time, she has choice. Zizi and Amalia are happy and send you their thanks.

Yours sincerely, Nathalie Oboke.

Birgit looked around the post office. The postmaster and his friend had resumed their conversation while Birgit, filled with curiosity at the strange writing, had torn open Nathalie's letter.

'How much is land around here?' she said and as they looked at her in silent surprise she said, 'I mean a plot, a small piece?'

They regarded her, weighing up her words.

She waved the thin blue paper, 'It's just that land in Africa seems so cheap.'

The postmaster spoke nodded towards a new cottage whose dormer windows were visible through the shop window,

'They say that half acre where the Dutchman built went for £25,000.'

'So much!'

''Tis the water. They'll pay any price for a bit of a view.'

Birgit looked at the other envelopes: from Oma and from Seán. She put all three into her pocket and went through the dark green door, pulling it shut to keep out the blustery wind that tore intermittently at the bare branches of the sycamore trees. She hurried back to her house, wanting to read Seán's letter in privacy.

It was dated January 21st.

Everything is in disarray, here. Your visit seems like
a mirage and as each day goes past with more trou-
bles than the last, I find it hard to believe that you
were ever here. I don't know how long I'll be here.
At present I am trying to make myself useful, driving for supplies (sometimes these are dropped
from the air and can land more or less anywhere
and are often scavenged by the time we find them)
and trying to keep order at the depot. That is what
the clinic has become. We *did* get it finished, so at
least it can be locked by night. Government troops
sometimes guard it against raiders. Who are the
raiders? Hungry people from other villages. By day
the women and old people and children arrive. By
night there are the raiders. I find myself so angry: if
we don't protect food supplies, children and their
parents whom we know, may starve. And yet, what
is the solution? The government doesn't like extra
foreigners here unless they are paramedics or other
people with 'relevant' skills, and apparently my jeep
(and my ability to keep it tanked up) count for
something.

How are you? (Rhetorical question. You can't
answer. Mail deliveries are definitely not a 'basic
essential'.) But I can imagine you reading this and
wanting to help. Well, there is something you can
do, for me at least. I spoke to my mother on the
phone. She sounded so faint and frail. She said it
was a bad line but I think she is unwell again. Please
go to see her. If she is all right then I can stay here

and keep trying.

Love, Seán.

p.s. Nathalie says she is writing to you. We work together at the depot sometimes but she hardly speaks to me. I don't know why but it could be she is just exhausted and worried out of her mind like everybody else. Her sisters have gone and her mother, believe it or not, is almost cheerful. She spoke to me for the first time in ages recently and wanted to know if you were coming back!

Birgit leaned against the stove, just lit, and waited for heat to come through its shining armour. The day was growing dark and though her lamps, paper, board and paints were ready, she found herself gazing into the twilight, hearing the wind whirl about the chimney but being unable to move, to find again the place in her mind, or the direction from it that had seemed obvious when she had earlier laid down her brush. She read Seán's letter again.

She glanced at Nathalie's: 'paid off' it seemed to say. After a long time she took her grandmother's letter from her pocket and slowly opened it.

20

Geoff was in the workshop, sitting at one end of the long bench with a hammer and tacks. While Simon prepared the stuffing for a large ornate Victorian chair, he was repairing a toy aeroplane. He picked up the propeller and tested the glued-on piece, pressing it to see if it was fully set. Satisfied, he slotted the propeller onto a tack and hammered it into the nose of the plane, leaving enough projecting for the propeller to move easily. Then he picked up the figure of a seated airman and glued on the head, pressing its broken neck together and wiping off the extruded glue. Then he held it in place in one hand and waited for the repair to dry. He looked at his watch. There had been no word from Olivia in the two days that had passed since Simon had spoken to Jenny, and more and more often he had wondered about the calls. Every time the phone rang, he found himself on the alert.

'Something the matter?' Simon, in a corner of the room, was sewing wadding together on a machine. Geoff had sat in one attitude for so long that Simon had felt an irresistible need to interrupt, to make sure that his father was not lost in the past and to have him sit up and focus those mild and thoughtful eyes on him.

'With me? No. And my friend here is well stuck, I'd say.' He touched the airman's head. 'No, I was wondering,' he stopped.

Here they were again having a calm conversation. The wonder of it distracted him.

'Yes?' Simon had paused with the needle half way through the fibre.

'I was wondering what's happened to Olivia.'

'Perhaps they are coming back?'

'I wish I knew. I wish –'

The airman lay unnoticed in his hand until he put it down and then, looking sideways towards the window, brought his hand up to rest his chin on it. This kind of silence, where his eyes darkened and his shoulders drooped, unnerved Simon. He pulled a tuft of wadding apart with a dry, rasping sound and, when Geoff remained still, said, 'What is it?'

'I was just trying to remember what she looked like.'

'Can't you –?'

'I have this photograph.'

Geoff slipped the small rectangle easily from his pocket. How often he had done that, since the day he had found the negative between the pages of one of Sadie's books. It was the old-fashioned kind, small, single. He had held it up to the light and had seen two figures: a woman in a long black dress and a man in a white suit, standing before an archway. The strangeness of it. The formal pose, so familiar. The woman was holding a spray of black flowers. Lilies? The man had a black flower in his lapel. A scrap of celluloid, keeping its own tawdry travesty of their wedding day, pressed like a flower between the pages of a book. One of those memories that he dreaded had advanced upon him, a day when, raging with grief, he tore all the family albums from the shelf in Sadie's sitting-room and burned them. Had this one negative fallen from the book to be saved by her and so carefully put away?

His heart had beaten painfully as he walked to the studio of the photographer down the street. The window was full of just such scenes, shining brides and flowery attendants, couples in dewy ovals, guests gathered on lawns beneath trees, all in colour. He was a kind man. He took one look at Geoff and led the way to his darkroom. Geoff had sat, he had had to sit, until the photographer brought the print still dripping, and reached towards the drying image with an absurd and desperate hope. It was not a good photograph. So very formal. He had wanted to say, 'But it can't have been like that!'

Simon came and stood beside him then bent down as he held up the photograph and looked at it.

'Is this all you have?'

Geoff nodded.

'Not very good, is it? Wait a minute.'

The words echoed and re-echoed as Simon left the shed. A faint draught moved through the loops of cord that hung from the ceiling as he waited. The footsteps hurried back and Geoff turned to see Simon bring a large green album and lay it on the bench, pushing the hammer and tacks aside to make room.

The wedding was there and the christenings and the holidays. Clare laughing as her veil ruffled forward like a swan's wing in front of her face; Clare trying not to laugh as the next photograph was taken and Geoff held down the wandering cloud of tulle; Clare distracted, glancing down for a moment as she leaned her head to hear him whisper something. The photographs were black and white but a carnival of colour and sound overwhelmed him. He could almost smell the lilies. He turned another page. Who was it who had christened the children? Vicar Brownlee. Old and slightly deaf. His voice had been a bit loud but it had suited the sonorities of the service. Another few pages of babies: how alike they looked when they were small but hers was the neater head. On the next page Rosie, face incredulous as a skin of shallow water slipped towards her bare feet: a pure childish incredulity, without premonition. The spade so large in her hand. Clare had written a caption: 'Water!' And under the next, where Rosie gazed in consternation at the ground: 'Sand!' She must have been one year old.

'Mob cap,' said Geoff suddenly. 'Wasn't that what they were called?'

Simon beside him had been looking from the book to his face and back to the book.

'I don't know. Is it?'

'Clare liked that sort of thing. Made them herself. For you too.'

He turned another page and went still. Simon waited, afraid to move.

'It was red,' said Geoff. 'A soft rose colour.'

He was looking at Rosie in a dress with short puffed sleeves and three small buttons below the collar.

'Oh?' Simon angled his head to see.

'You'd have been seven then, don't you remember?'

'Not really. The photographs make me realize that I must have remembered, once. Sadie kept that album by her bed and every night we'd sit down and look through it. Somewhere along the way, the real recollection was overtaken by the photographs. You know? Like when you read a book and then, much later, see the film and the film gets in the way of your own memory, so there's always a sort of double image?'

Simon touched the corner of the album. 'You must take it.'

'I can't. It's all you have.'

'I have all those photographs in my head. If I never saw them again, I'd have every one incised in my mind's eye.'

More footsteps came, muffled through the grass, then clear on the flagstone steps. Becky put her head around the door.

'It's for you, Geoff. The phone.'

Jenny spoke without preliminaries. 'We're on our way back. We'll be home tomorrow evening.'

He stood very still. Did that mean afternoon or night?

'That's great,' he tried, then, 'isn't it?'

'Not really. Olivia's not well. She – well, you'll see for yourself. Listen, someone's waiting to use the phone.'

'What can I do for you?'

'See that the house is OK. Warm. It needs to be very warm.'

'Anything else?'

'No. Just drop in if you have time. She's worried about you, for some reason, and she has enough to bother her without worrying about you!'

There was a trace of flirtation in her voice. Perhaps things were not so bad.

He laid the receiver in its cradle and turned to Becky.

'I must go.'

'Go?' She paused and specks of flour fell off her arms into the mixing bowl.

'Home. I'll have to get the place ready for them.' She continued to regard him.

'But –'

'Olivia's not well. Ill. How ill I don't know but they're on their way back.'

'When?'

'Tomorrow.'

She rubbed her hands slowly, watching the brief clouds of flour puff and die. 'Are you really ready to –' she looked about, 'to do so much?'

But she could see that he was. He stood straight. He looked at her with polite patience.

'It's not much and they need me.' His attention was now fixed upon her. 'You have been so good to me.'

'It's not that.'

'And I'm ready to pull myself together.'

'I didn't mean –'

He moved towards the table. 'I'm welcome here, I know that. Isn't that right?'

She relaxed.

'You've been so good to me.' He corrected himself. 'You've never been anything but good to me. So good I take it for granted, as I shouldn't.'

She smiled.

Simon drove him to the bookshop and while the engine turned over at the door, reached into the back seat, brought forward the album and put it into Geoff's hands.

'If I want to see it, I'll know who to ask.'

After he had checked the central heating and turned it up, he lit a fire in the sitting-room and opened the windows. The field beyond the river was empty of cattle and great pools of water made gleaming discs in the fading light. The river was running fast with branches and debris stuck at the brink, the crooks of limbs sticking up like elbows. A cloud of starlings flickered and whirled up to the hills, back to the trees, down to the river. The house was spotless except for the kitchen where the decanter stopper had left a sticky mark on the white worktop. He found a cloth and bleach and scrubbed at the stain.

In the decanter, the port vibrated. He stood up and brought the moment when he had tasted it clearly into his mind. Horrible. He made a last swirl with the cloth leaving still a pinkish sickle. The glass. What would he say about the glass? He rinsed out the cloth and held it to his forehead. The cold made his forehead ache and suddenly he felt uneasy, nervous of the return, aware that someone reliable and decent would be needed, not a half-redeemed alcoholic who would steal their booze, break their glass and then throw it away to hide the fact. He wanted to sit down, to reassume old age, to let Becky fold him in warmth and kindness, to have Simon watch him with that nervous alertness that was more moving than any attempt at a reconciliation. He looked at his watch. Too late: they would be here soon.

He went to the shop to look out and as he closed the door, caught sight of himself in a pier glass at the far side of the room: an old man with a white beard. He put up his hand and touched it: stubble, bristle, not a real beard, just unshaven. They would be shocked. The jangle of the shop bell was a distraction. He reached up and hooked it back, then went quickly into his own house.

It was more difficult than he remembered. The stubble was very tough and resistant to the old soap-clogged blade. Hacking away with it, he made a couple of small cuts on his jaw. He found a new blade and, hurrying now to insert it in the razor, nicked his thumb. He swore, ran water on the cut then finished the shave with a slow delta of blood spreading down his bare arm, like an external vein, to soak into the rolled sleeve of his shirt. He stuck paper on the cuts and put a plaster on his thumb and wiped off the blood. Then he pulled on the green jumper and found that it covered the bloodied shirt. He carefully unpeeled the scraps of paper without opening the wounds. Then he stood back and looked in the mirror. Raw blotches marked his face and the cuts looked like badges of disrepute. He tidied his hair and, when it caught the light, leaned forward to peer at his reflection. There could be no doubt about it, the golden strands were run through very definitely with grey. Long grey hairs, not merely faded but hairs that had obviously been growing for months. The contrast between his hair and face was no longer ludicrous. If it was plain to him then it must have been plain to others for some time.

Quickly he went downstairs, pausing to look again at the clean, neat kitchen. Not a bottle in sight (or out of it), not a festering tin or ashtray: a spray of some white flower in a glass on the table. Becky, Simon. Both of them.

He took the glass and went next door and set it on the low table in front of the fire in the sitting-room: in the larger space, it looked overwhelmed and sad, a proof of winter's harshness. He moved it to the mantelpiece where its reflection doubled the blossoms: a pleasant deception. He checked the fire and took the guard off to make the room more welcoming. He looked at his watch again. He started to worry. He drew the curtains and stood at the fire, then remembered that he had tied up the bell and hurried downstairs.

The evening traffic was beginning to thin out but still exhaust steam made lurid clouds under the streetlights. He willed the street to empty so that when the car came, it could sweep across and pull up, unhindered, on the pavement. Not wanting to let chill, noxious air in, he went inside and closed the door again and stood waiting in the lamplight with the ticking of various clocks working on his nerves. A big truck edged past with a shuddering load of coal and gas followed by a cloud of diesel through which, at last, loomed their car.

He rushed out to hold the car door as Jenny struggled onto the pavement, flapping her hand before her face. 'What a welcome!' she coughed. 'Don't mind me. See to Olivia.' He went to the passenger door which Olivia had just started to open. She smiled up at him.

'Geoff!' she said. 'How lovely to see you.' There was relief in her voice. Very slowly, she levered herself out of the car and as he helped her, he tried not to show his dismay. She seemed to have shrunk. The yellow streetlights made her look like a discoloured paper ornament. In the back of the car was a wheelchair. She saw him glance away from it.

'Oh, that.' She lifted her hand dismissively, a fan of bones. 'That's just for airports and things. It's not necessary. Just to keep Jenny happy, more than anything.'

They sat around the table in the kitchen and Jenny poured out the soup.

'And bread and cheese and salad. You've thought of everything,' she said to Geoff.

But Olivia ate nothing and could manage to drink only a small bowl of soup.

'Too tired to be hungry,' she said, and Jenny did not contradict her.

They sat at the fire when Olivia had gone to bed: taking a few steps up the stairs and then pausing to rest. She refused help and Jenny did not try to persuade her.

'It's no use,' said Jenny after a while. 'Of course she should be in the chair and she should not climb the stairs and so on and on and on, but believe me, it was she who decided to come home. I'd have pushed her up Mont bloody Blanc in that chair, if she'd let me.'

'She wanted to come home?'

'Yes.'

'She looks so –' he could not find a suitable word and regretted having tried.

'Wasted?'

'Mm.' He was surprised at her cool accuracy.

'This has happened before. Each time it gets a bit worse but she copes. She really believes she'll get better. I dread the day when she accepts that she won't.'

There was silence and then she turned her head from the fire to him. 'Do you know what I'd really love? A drink. A lovely, calm, warm glass of wine.'

208

As he reached the door she added, 'Just bring a bottle from under the stairs. The glasses are here.'

He uncorked the bottle and placed it on the hearth, then turned to choose a glass from the miscellany on the side table. The engraved goblet stood by itself. He paused then, taking a breath, picked it up and brought it across the room to her.

'One glass?'

'I broke the other,' he said suddenly.

'Oh?' she seemed uninterested, then glanced sharply at him, then away to the bottle, then down to the glass in her hand. Then she sat up, reached out and flicked the glass into the hearth. Dazed, he watched. She sat back and raised her eyebrows: 'Quits?'

He said nothing. His confession refused to take shape.

'I think I can guess,' she said, 'but spare me the explanations, please.'

He sat down. 'I'm sorry –'

'No. You gave us a wonderful welcome, don't spoil it.'

She closed her eyes for a moment and he was reminded of Olivia in the exhaustion scored on her face. Without that burden he could imagine she would be as beautiful.

'The flowers.' She had opened her eyes. 'They are what?'

He shrugged. 'No idea.'

When she had finished her wine, she yawned and he stood up.

'You know where to find me, if you need me at any time?'

She smiled. 'It's a comfort that, knowing you are there.' She jerked her head towards the wall they shared.

In his bedroom, he took off the green jumper and draped it on a chair, then picked up the bottle of tablets, unscrewed it and shook two into his palm. Could he risk dreams, those random attacks that left him shaking, choking, calling out? And if he were needed during the night? A nightmare would now disturb only him. He put one pill next to the glass of water as a prompt or a fail-safe. Then he lay down and thought about the flowers. The name would not come but the chilly petals clustered on the spiny branches, so tenacious, so contemptuous of winter, blossomed fixedly before his eyes.

21

Dear Oma,

Your letter has come at last and I was happy to read of your wonderful adventures. I wish I had been there to see you skiing.

And so Peter is married: that photograph! Yes, it did make me laugh and of course it was in the newspapers. The daughter of a Judge, well! No wonder he smiles like a pumpkin. You think she is plump but in that dress she looks just pleasantly curvy, and yes, she is smiling like the cat who got the cream, so they are both happy.

It was good to have something cheerful because life here has been quite sad. My neighbour Jerome died suddenly and now there are fewer people in the post office. The loss of even one person makes a big difference to the island. He should have been buried on the mainland and then Margaret would have gone there to live but instead he was buried just a few miles away, on Oileán Cré, and Margaret is so glad. I see her very often. She comes to sit for her portrait. She is the best sitter in the world, usually. She can be still for hours, looking inward to her

memories but every now and again she suddenly
breaks out with some comment, like today: 'He
wouldn't have been himself next to that old famine
grave.' I almost dropped my brush. She said there is
a huge plot in the town cemetery where hundreds
of people were buried last century. Jerome hated it
and would never go near it. Foolishly, I asked about
the roofless and derelict houses here and on the
other islands. She was outraged. 'There was never
famine on the islands. Never!' You should have seen
her. She was quivering with rage. It took a long time
for her to become calm. How I wish I could paint
all those moods, the sudden changes, the movement of her thoughts causing her face to go on fire
and those eyes to burn. Yet even when she is calm,
her eyes are alight and I wonder what thoughts are
contained behind them, unspoken. If I am ever to
learn about this place, I will have to be very careful.
I will have to listen so hard to what she says and
what she does not say. For now, all she will say is,
'Jerome knew all about that,' but some time, she
may tell me. Meanwhile, I shall have to keep her
calm, if there is ever to be a portrait.

You were right. I did not need to keep my drawing of Geoff just because it was the best thing I had
done. You didn't tell me to burn it but that was
what I did and I don't regret it. The flames con-
sumed my drawing and with it some of my shame.
Perhaps I will try to make a portrait of him next, he
has an interesting face, full of sympathy. I have seen
him often recently, as we both visit Seán's mother,
and he encourages me to paint.

I had a note, you could not call it a letter, from Seán. The rains did not come and he is helping to feed people. It sounds very bad.

As for myself, I will stay here. I think I have found something: the end or the beginning of something, I don't know which. I feel 'founded' in this place which has so much hidden under its brilliant surface.

Margaret and I have two projects: the completion of her portrait and the repair of the churchyard wall. We will stay indoors creating her painting together, until the weather grows warm and then, perhaps after Easter, we will go to Oileán Cré with our shovels and start to rebuild the sea wall, stone by stone.

Today, February 1st, is the beginning of spring (this is the land of optimists) and the Feast Day of my Patron Saint: is that not auspicious? So summer begins in May. Come and visit then. We will swim among sea-birds, seals and fish and you will see that I am not, as they say here, 'out of my mind', but 'in my element'.

Fondest love, Birgit.

The preliminary drawings were done. Margaret, in her blue housecoat, was sitting with her profile to the light, the cool north light that showed every line of her face. Her hands were folded on her lap and the yellow mug from which she had drunk was still warm on the table beside her. Next to it, the colours in their dented tubes were laid out in five rows and a fresh jar of water with a trickle down its side had been placed beside them. In it

the surface still slopped gently. Birgit picked up a large brush and
dipped it in the water.

22

When you have lost your memory you have no control over the past. You cannot order its events to please yourself or even to decide what was true, or worth remembering. You are haunted by what is not. It is a vacuum that grows and grows until it has absorbed everything and left you with nothing. I sometimes wonder why I didn't kill myself: it would have been so tidy, it would finally have made something. Another mess for someone to clean up, I know, I know, but at the end of Christmas Day when a mirror to the haphazard perfections of life had been held up and then smashed, I saw only darkness. While I drank, there was either a half-light or that unreal light that one might see from the depths of a tank, or just the dark. And dark was best. If I had been going to kill myself I would have bought a few crates of whiskey and made a proper job of it. One bottle a day showed a kind of optimism, a hope that annihilation would just sneak up on me, or maybe that I would be rescued. I can still remember its comforts: when I was really drunk, nothing else mattered.

But when I regained my memory, I had no control over that either. The endless repetitions made me terrified of sleep and yet, during the day, waves and droves of jostling images like refugees, starving, fleeing the past, clamoured for attention. If, sitting in the window seat at Simon's house, I closed my eyes in the sun, I would see the pink of blood diluted not by light but by water. If I sat in the car, I could not turn my head for fear of seeing small fingers clutching the back of the seat. If Stevie leaned against me I wanted to grasp him, to save him from, from what? Life? Death? Or that which joins them: danger. It is such a selfish thing, grief, it reduces everything to a prompt of memory, hissing and nagging in the wings.

I was terrified of everything and yet I was more terrified of revealing that terror. So I hid it because I couldn't explain. Now there was another loss, something I had had and it was gone. And then one day I realized that I no longer needed to define things in words because all I had been doing, before that moment on Inis Breac, was marking time and trying to contain it: to contrive memories. But what is memory without light and colour and feeling? I'm not sad that those sterile syllables no longer click into place like the tumblers of a safe. I can lean my head to watch the sunlight fall at a different angle in the shop window, or rise every day at dawn to see the layers of mist on the river thin and fade. I can catch Stevie in my arms and throw him in the air when he rushes up and flings himself at me and I can hold Tom's shoulders as he bends over the wall to count the purple urchins in the lake. I can weed vegetables for Becky and make repairs for Simon. Make repairs: how apt.

And I can help Olivia. We brought her bed down to the sitting-room and she lies there most of the day watching the river, counting moorhens, charting the movement of the starlings, watching the flooded fields and hoping for a time when the pasture will be full of cattle again: black and white cows and, always, one brown one. They keep up brave and cheerful faces for one another but sometimes, when Olivia is asleep, Jenny will slump into a chair in the kitchen and say she does not know what to do. At other times Olivia will say, 'I don't know what will become of Jenny.'

But while I am needed, I'll keep sitting with her; or look for early daffodils with their green buds to bring her, reading from her favourite books or just watching the river, and who knows, maybe by summer she will be better and this hard spring will have been just another stage.

It sounds so tidy, so well rounded. Everything in its place. A few adjustments here, a grain of homely philosophy there and the pathetic, ageing former drunk looks well set to become the picture-book granddad. Even the hair has made a truce, a graceful acceptance of the silver, an acknowledgment that the gold is better placed elsewhere. But words, those tiny pointed weapons, like the stakes the Lilliputians used to anchor Gulliver to the sand, can yet shake all that new-found happiness.

Birgit asked me for advice. She arrived at the antique shop when I was saying goodbye to Olivia one afternoon and then appeared at my door soon afterwards. I made coffee, as I always do when she calls, busying myself with the mechanics of the thing: a new packet to open, the kettle to refill and so on, the little clichés of the inarticulate, to prolong her stay. She did not wander along the shelves, chattering, as she usually does, she just sat on the edge of the centre table with her head down and when I brought the mug she took it and placed it beside her.

'What should I do?' she said.

I was at a loss. If pedantic musings about words had made life containable, they had also distanced them. Their actual utterance was unpractised. I just stared at her.

'Olivia says I should not visit. She says she has Jenny and you. She does not want to take my time.'

If I agreed with her, I would lose her. I continued to stare.

'She says I may call if I am in town but not to come specially. She was not unkind, not unfriendly, oh, you must not think so.'

She had started to gabble, to fill the silence.

'So what am I to do? Olivia is, she says, getting better, my grandmother is independent, I cannot help Seán or Nathalie ...' She reeled off a list of names from her travels. 'Margaret's portrait is almost done and anyway, painting ... What use is painting?'

Another time I might have laughed. Well, at least rhetorical questions don't need answers. And then she was off again, talking about selfishness. But if I shared my expertise on that subject with her, she would flee, and rightly. By now she was pacing the floor, her plait swinging like a tiger's tail, as she scolded herself. I watched it catch the light when she turned, and tried to think of something to say. You rescued me, I thought, and now you are asking me ... Don't ask.

The blizzard of words continued. I closed my eyes. 'Women at the Well', 'Charlie and his Pliers', 'Children under the School Tree' whirled past me and I imagined that I could see them. I opened my eyes and they vanished, no match for her feline pacing. And then I realized that I had seen them, all around the walls of her kitchen. Suddenly she stopped.

'You think I am a mad woman.'

'No.'

She leaned against a bookshelf, raised one hand and let the backs of her fingers trail across the spines of the books. I opened my cigarettes and took one out.

'I'll have one too.'

The little busyness of offering the packet and lighting the cigarette being another of those handy stratagems, I made the most of it. She grimaced and blew out smoke as I offered a few words.

'They are good.'

'What?'

'Your paintings.'

She raised her eyebrows and frowned at me and then looked at one that she had given me: a man in a waterhole putting a basin

218

on the edge, stretching up his arms, and in the background, a frail row of onions, the only colour, the only note of hope in his solitary toil. I cannot describe the pleasure it gave me to frame it and the twinge of recognition I felt every time I looked at it.

'You think?'

The ash grew on her cigarette as she stared at the painting. This was not the time to repeat the conversation that I had overheard the previous day between two customers.

'Mm, it's ...' one said.

'Childish?' said the other.

'Not exactly. More sort of – I know, primitive!'

'Dad might like it. He's into native art.'

Of course I'd said it was not for sale.

I handed Birgit an ashtray.

'I ask too much of you,' she said

'You couldn't do that.' It said itself before I could stop it.

'Oh?'

The quietness with which she said it made it seem perilous. Inarticulacy became my ally.

'I think ... well ... you see ...'

She waited.

'It's just that every time I pass that painting, I cannot, I mean I cannot pass it without looking. And so many people have asked about it.'

She looked back at the picture.

'Perhaps that is enough.'

She is to bring in her paintings and I am to frame them. Though it is not for sale, I put the onion grower in the window after she left and looked at it from across the street.

That evening I took down the album for my daily visit to the past, the ordered past. The chaos of sensation that had at first flown up from the photographs had become muted. I found myself turning the last few pages without lingering. I know all those images. They are mine.

I started to design a new sign for the shop: 'Books & Paintings', or 'Paintings & Books'; maybe even 'Gallery'? I'll see how it goes.